Benjamin Orange Flower

Whittier

Prophet, Seer and Man

Benjamin Orange Flower

Whittier
Prophet, Seer and Man

ISBN/EAN: 9783337034054

Printed in Europe, USA, Canada, Australia, Japan

Cover: Foto ©Raphael Reischuk / pixelio.de

More available books at **www.hansebooks.com**

WHITTIER.

WORKS BY B. O. FLOWER.

THE CENTURY OF SIR THOMAS
MORE. (Illustrated.) Fancy cloth, - $1.50

PERSONS, PLACES AND IDEAS: Mis-
cellaneous Essays. (Richly illustrated.) Cloth, - - - - - - - - - $3.00

GERALD MASSEY: Poet, Prophet and
Mystic. (Illustrated.) Cloth, - - - $1.00

CIVILIZATION'S INFERNO; or, Studies
in the Social Cellar. Cloth, - - - - $1.00

THE NEW TIME: A Plea for the Union
of the Moral Forces for Freedom and
Progress. Cloth, - - - - - - - - $1.00

LESSONS LEARNED FROM OTHER
LIVES: A Book of Short Biographies
for Young People. Cloth, - - - - - $1.00

WHITTIER: Prophet, Seer and Man.
(With frontispiece.) Cloth, - - - - $1.00

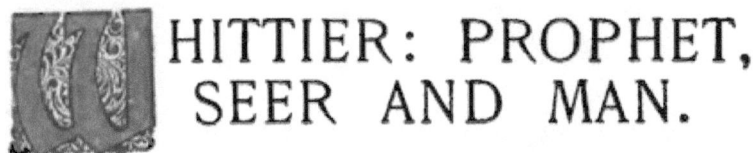

WHITTIER: PROPHET, SEER AND MAN.

WITH PORTRAIT.

✦

By B. O. FLOWER, AUTHOR OF
"THE CENTURY OF SIR THOMAS MORE,"
"GERALD MASSEY," "CIVILIZATION'S
INFERNO," "THE NEW TIME," ETC.

✦

THE ARENA PUBLISHING
CO., BOSTON, MASS.
MDCCCXCVI.

ARENA PRESS.

THIS VOLUME IS
AFFECTIONATELY DEDICATED TO
MY NIECE,

Gertrude M. Binley,

WHOSE BRIGHT, THOUGHTFUL,
AND SINCERE NATURE HAS
ENDEARED HER TO ALL
WHO KNOW HER.

CONTENTS.

INTRODUCTION.

failed to live up to their fine teachings and, in unguarded moments and hours of temptation, have so fallen that the recollection of their shortcomings rests like a sable cloud over their noble utterances. Not so with Whittier; his life was exceptionally pure, and while I imagine no man ever reaches at all times his ideals, our Quaker poet, in a greater degree than most of us, maintained that serenity of soul, that purity of thought and kindliness of nature, which reflect the divine side of man. That he sometimes fell short of his high ideals, is shown in many of his own lines, notably in the following from "My Triumph:"

> Let the thick curtain fall ;
> I better know than all
> How little I have gained,
> How vast the unattained.
>
> * * * *
>
> Sweeter than any sung,
> My songs that found no tongue ;
> Nobler than any fact,
> My wish which failed of act.

And this consciousness of a failure to live up to his own highest level in thought and aspiration is further illustrated in the following touching story told by Mrs. Mary B. Claflin, in her "Personal Recollections of Whittier:"

"The morning mail," observes this lady, "usually brought him a great number of letters (often as many as fifty); and one morning as he was looking over the pile before him, he lingered a long time over one, and looked troubled, as though it contained some sad news. At length handing it to me, he said: 'I wish thee would read that letter;' and then, with his head downcast, and his deep, melancholy eyes looking, as it seemed, into the very depths of human mysteries, he sat still till I had finished it.

"It was written by one whose life had been spent on a remote farm among the hills of New Hampshire, away from every privilege her nature craved—a most pathetic letter written, it seemed, out of the deepest human longing for sympathy, for companionship and uplifting. The lonely woman wrote, she said, to tell Mr. Whittier what his poems had been to her during all the years of her desolate heart-yearning for education, for enlightenment, and for touch with the great outside world. She added: ' In my darkest moments I have found light and comfort in your poems, which I always keep by my side; and as I never expect to have the privilege of looking into your face, I feel that I must tell you, before I leave this world, what you have been through your writings to one and, I have no doubt, to many a longing heart and homesick soul. I have never been in a place so dark and hopeless that I could not find light and comfort and hope in your poems ; and when I go into my small room and close my door upon the worries and perplexing cares that constantly beset me, and sit down by my window that looks out over the hills, which have been my only companions, I never fail to find in the volume, which is always by my side, some word of peace and comfort to my longing heart.'

"The letter was such as would bring tears from any sympathetic heart, and I remarked, returning it to him, 'I would rather have the testimony you are constantly receiving from forlorn and hungry souls— the assurance that you are helping God's neglected children—than the crown of any queen on earth.'

"With tearful eyes and choking voice, he replied : 'Such letters greatly humiliate me. I can sometimes write from a high plane, but thee knows I cannot live up to it all the time. I wish I could think I deserved all the kind things said of me.'"

This touching incident is thoroughly characteristic of the life of one in whom we find humility, sincerity, simplicity, sympathy, only equalled by a passionate devotion to freedom, justice, and truth—a man who was at once a poet of nature, an apostle of liberty, and a prophet of progress. He interpreted in a manner 'thoroughly intelligible to the most unschooled mind the profoundest truths of life, which pertain to the spirit, and which come only to the mystic, who in the hushed chambers of his soul hears speak the still, small voice of the Infinite. Finally, and crowning all, his life, of which I have spoken, was such as to give special emphasis to his inspired lines, conferring on them a peculiar value for aspiring youth.

A BAREFOOT BOY WHO WAS
ALSO A DREAMER.

.

"Blessings on thee, little man,
    Barefoot boy, with cheek of tan !
    With thy turned-up pantaloons,
    And thy merry whistled tunes;
    With thy red lip, redder still
    Kissed by strawberries on the hill;
    With the sunshine on thy face,
    Through thy torn brim's jaunty grace;
    From my heart I give thee joy,—
    I was once a barefoot boy!"
                —*Whittier's " Barefoot Boy."*

"I think at the age of which thy note inquires, I found about equal satisfaction in an old rural home with the shifting panorama of seasons, in reading the few books within my reach, *and in dreaming of something wonderful and grand in the future.*"
                —*Whittier to a youthful correspondent.*

I. A Barefoot Boy who was also a Dreamer.

OHN GREENLEAF WHITTIER was born on the 17th of December, 1807, in a typical New England farmhouse, a short distance from the town of Haverhill, in Massachusetts. His father was poor; rigid economy and incessant toil on the part of all members of the household were required in order to provide life's necessities and lift a debt which hung over the dear old homestead. If, however, the little Quaker boy was schooled in poverty, it cannot be said that he was poor in any other sense than that he possessed little of that which gold may purchase. As a matter of fact, few children enter the arena

3

of life so dowered with inestimable riches as the little barefoot boy, who was destined to become New England's poet of home life and America's prophet of freedom. Behind him were generations of pure, high-minded and sturdy ancestors. In his parents we find united the rare charm which marks the life of the consistent and profoundly religious Quaker and the sturdy, almost austere morality of the Puritan shorn, however, of that harsh, unrelenting and intolerant spirit which not unfrequently shadowed and made repulsive the otherwise noble lives of the early Puritans.

Nor were the hereditary influences and prenatal conditions more favorable than the environment that enclosed his early years. Biographers have frequently deplored the poverty of Whittier's parents, which prevented the youth from having access to many books adapted to the young; but I am by no means convinced that this apparent misfortune was not a blessing, rather than an evil. Many of the men who have accomplished most for the moral uplift and enduring progress of the race have had access to but few books in youth. Indeed, the studious child who possesses few books soon assimilates their contents and unconsciously acquires the habit of retaining the facts which have been drawn from their pages, in a manner quite unknown to those who are surfeited with literature and who early learn to skim over rather than carefully peruse a printed page; and this early acquired habit of retaining facts remains with the person throughout life. Again, the thoughtful and ambitious child whose literature is so limited that he soon masters the knowledge contained in the books within his reach early turns his mind in other directions in search of knowledge; he becomes a close observer of Nature and, if possessed of imagination, the sky, earth and sea, the changing seasons,

the forest and the flowers, the birds and bees
—each of these bears a message to his brain.
We must also remember that the child who
from early youth has been surrounded by
books comes to rely too much on the opinion
and thoughts of others, and loses an originality in idea and expression which has never
been properly fostered by educational pro-
cesses. This, fortunately, Whittier escaped;
what he lacked in book-learning was more
than made up by—

Knowledge never learned of schools,
Of the wild bee's morning chase,
Of the wild-flower's time and place,
Flight of fowl, and habitude
Of the tenants of the wood;
How the tortoise bears his shell,
How the woodchuck digs his cell,
And the ground-mole sinks his well;
How the robin feeds her young,
How the oriole's nest is hung;
Where the whitest lilies blow,
Where the freshest berries grow,
Where the groundnut trails its vine,
Where the wood-grape's clusters shine;

Of the black wasp's cunning way,
Mason of his walls of clay,
And the architectural plans
Of gray hornet artisans !

Nature teaches those children who will hearken to her words, and she is never false in word or note or picture. If the literature of the Whittier family was very limited, she was prodigal with treasures which appealed to the eye, ear and imagination of the Quaker boy.

I was rich in flowers and trees,
Humming birds and honey bees;
For my sport the squirrel played,
Plied the snouted mole his spade;
For my taste the blackberry cone
Purpled over hedge and stone;
Laughed the brook for my delight
Through the day and through the night,
Whispering at the garden wall,
Talked with me from fall to fall;
Mine the sand-rimmed pickerel pond,
Mine the walnut slopes beyond,
Mine on bending orchard trees
Apples of Hesperides !
Still as my horizon grew,
Larger grew my riches, too.

Whittier never lost sight of the treasures which were his amid what men of to-day would term biting poverty. On one occasion when casting a retrospective glance over the long vanished past, he thus characterized his early lot:

A farmer's son,
Proud of field-lore and harvest craft, and feeling
All their fine possibilities, how rich
And restful even poverty and toil
Become when beauty, harmony, and love
Sit at their humble hearth as angels sat
At evening in the Patriarch's tent, when man
Makes labor noble !

The old homestead of the Whittier family has been endeared to the nation by the many bits of descriptive verse which the poet has woven into his poems of New England life. It was a large frame building somewhat better than the average farmhouse of the period. Around it grew a variety of hardy trees, such as maple, walnut, butternut, and the picturesque Lombardy poplar.

In one of his prose sketches the poet thus describes the site of the old home :

"It was surrounded by woods in all directions save to the southeast, where a break in the leafy wall revealed a vista of low green meadows, picturesque with wooded islands and jutting capes of upland; through these a small brook, noisy enough as it foamed, rippled and laughed down the rocky falls. By our garden side wound silently and scarcely visible a still larger stream known as the Country Brook."

Rising abruptly almost from the Whittier garden was Job's Hill, a lofty eminence from which a magnificent view of the surrounding country could be obtained, although the height was not so favorable in this respect as Great Hill, a little distance further on. It was on the slope of Job's Hill that the young poet when quite small suddenly found himself confronted with great peril, from which he was saved only by what in a human being we should call presence of mind, on the part of a favorite ox named Old Butler. Mr. Samuel T. Pickard, whose "Life and Letters of Whittier" is the latest and most authoritative utterance on the life of the poet, thus describes this interesting incident:

"One side of Job's hill is exceedingly steep—too steep for such an unwieldy animal as an ox to descend rapidly in safety. Greenleaf went to the pasture one day with a bag of salt for the cattle, and Old Butler from the brow of the hill recognized him and knew his errand. As the boy was bent over, shaking the salt out of the bag, the ox came down the hill towards him with flying leaps, and his speed was so great that he could not check himself. He would have crushed his young master, but by a supreme effort, gathering himself together at the right moment, the noble creature leaped straight into the air, over the head of the boy, and came to the ground far below with a tremendous concussion and without serious injury to himself."

The same author gives an additional anecdote about this favorite ox, as related by Mr. Whittier:

"Quaker meetings were sometimes held in the large kitchen at his father's house. One summer day, on such an occasion, this ox had the curiosity to put his head in at the open window and take a survey of the assembly. While a sweet-voiced woman was speaking, Old Butler paid strict attention, but when she sat down and there arose a loud-voiced brother, the ox withdrew his head from the window, lifted his tail in air and went off bellowing. This bovine criticism was greatly enjoyed by the younger members of the meeting."

The most important room in the old homestead, as it was lovingly called by the poet, was the kitchen, immortalized in "Snow-Bound;" but, besides this room, on the ground floor were other apartments, one of which was always regarded somewhat as a sanctuary by the children and was known as "mother's room." On the second floor were several chambers which possess special interest for lovers of the poet. In one of these the young poet made his experiment in lifting, which Trowbridge has so aptly described in one of his delightful little poems. The story is as follows: One day during the working hours young John, musing on the fact that he found no difficulty in lifting his brother Matt, and that his brother had also frequently lifted *him*, came to the conclusion that, if the two lifted together, both would simultaneously rise. This conclusion, it will be seen, although plausible on its face, like so many things in

life which involve factors that have not
been considered was destined to prove a dis-
appointment to the youthful experimenter.
The poet imparted his deductions to his
brother, who thought them reasonable, and
forthwith the experiment was tried in their
room. Somehow it did not work, but as
Trowbridge observes:

> 'Twas a shrewd notion none the less,
> And still, in spite of ill success,
>   It somehow has succeeded.
> Kind Nature smiled on that wise child,
>   Nor could her love deny him
> The large fulfilment of his plan;
> Since he who lifts his brother man
>   In turn is lifted by him.

Whittier was an ethical philosopher rather
than a scientist, and the idea he conceived
was neither false nor unphilosophical in the
ethical realm, or world of conduct, as his
own life illustrates.

Many of those most delightful pictures of

New England life which were indelibly impressed upon the sensitive plate of his brain, at this time when nature taught the artless boy, hold for us a special charm, due to their revealing the secret hopes, loves and disappointments which entered into his life. While it is probable that Whittier does not reproduce in detail actual experiences when he reveals to us love welling high in his heart—for pictures of this character are usually held sacred and carefully guarded from an unsympathetic world, even when the profound emotions which they awaken lend power to the flights of the imagination —there can be little doubt but that he experienced every emotion which he so simply and beautifully depicts. Thus, when we read the following exquisite lines from " My Playmate," we see behind the moaning pines on Ramoth Hill, the falling blossoms eddying in the fitful breeze, the melody of the robin's song or the gay plumage of the oriole, beyond the violet-sprinkled sod, beyond the graceful waving branches of the birch, beyond all these beauties and melodies of Nature, the workings of the human heart; we catch a glimpse of something which is always sacred, something in the presence of which "the soul kneels though the body may remain erect," and that something is the Holy of Holies of the human heart from which the poet for a moment lifts the veil : *(My Playmate)*

> The pines were dark on Ramoth Hill,
>   Their song was soft and low ;
> The blossoms in the sweet May wind
>   Were falling like the snow.
>
> The blossoms drifted at our feet,
>   The orchard birds sang clear ;
> The sweetest and the saddest day
>   It seemed of all the year.
>
> For, more to me than birds or flowers,
>   My playmate left her home,
> And took with her the laughing spring,
>   The music and the bloom.

She kissed the lips of kith and kin,
  She laid her hand in mine :
What more could ask the bashful boy
  Who fed her father's kine ?

She left us in the bloom of May;
  The constant years told o'er
Their seasons with as sweet May morns,
  But she came back no more.

She lives where all the golden year
  Her summer roses blow ;
The dusky children of the sun
  Before her come and go.

There, haply, with her jewelled hands
  She smooths her silken gown—
No more the homespun lap wherein
  I shook the walnuts down.

I see her face, I hear her voice—
  Does she remember mine ?
And what to her is now the boy
  Who fed her father's kine ?

What cares she that the orioles build
  For other eyes than ours,—
That other hands with nuts are filled,
  And other laps with flowers ?

O playmate in the golden time !
  Our mossy seat is green,
Its fringing violets blossom yet,
  The old trees o'er it lean,

The winds so sweet with birch and fern
  A sweeter memory blow,
And there in spring the veeries sing
  The song of long ago.

And still the pines of Ramoth wood
  Are moaning like the sea,—
The moaning of the sea of change
  Between myself and thee !

Again, these simple but natural lines have won their way into the hearts of English-speaking people, because in them our poet, in picturing a boyhood scene, has imbued it with sentiment so delicately expressed and so true, that the heart of humanity, being one, responds to that which recalls youth's sweet dream, when for the first time all things are glorified with the indefinable rapture of love's awakening :

Still sits the schoolhouse by the road,
  A ragged beggar sunning ;
Around it still the sumachs grow,
  And blackberry vines are running.

Within, the master's desk is seen,
  Deep scarred by raps official;
The warping floor, the battered seats,
  The jackknife's carved initial;

The charcoal frescos on its wall;
  Its door's worn sill, betraying
The feet that, creeping slow to school,
  Went storming out to playing !

Long years ago a winter sun
  Shone over it at setting;
Lit up its western window panes,
  And low eaves' icy fretting.

It touched the tangled, golden curls
  And brown eyes, full of grieving,
Of one who still her steps delayed
  When all the school were leaving.

For near her stood the little boy
  Her childish favor singled,
His cap pulled low upon a face
  Where pride and shame were mingled.

Pushing with restless feet the snow
　　To right and left, he lingered,
As restlessly her tiny hands
　　The blue-checked apron fingered.

He saw her lift her eyes ; he felt
　　The soft hand's light caressing,
And heard the tremble of her voice,
　　As if a fault confessing :

" I'm sorry that I spelt the word ;
　　I hate to go above you,
Because," —the brown eyes lower fell,—
　　" Because, you see, I love you!"

Still memory to a gray-haired man
　　That sweet child-face is showing.
Dear girl! the grasses on her grave
　　Have forty years been growing !

He lives to learn, in life's hard school,
　　How few who pass above him
Lament their triumph and his loss,
　　Like her,—because they love him.

But of all the poems descriptive of child
life and New England scenes and incidents
which were absorbed by his plastic brain
while he was still a boy and destined to be
marvellously developed in later years, none

equals that superb idyl of the old-time New England winter, " Snow-Bound." In this creation we have some wonderfully faithful pictures, almost photographic in quality, although to a certain extent idealized. " Snow-Bound " was written in 1866; it was the first important work produced by the poet after he had exchanged the helmet of the aggressive reformer for the robe of the poet-priest of nature. And in this counterfeit presentment of his childhood's home during that memorable New England winter we see a subtle and almost indefinable idealization which might be compared to the purple mantle which rests over the distant hills at eventide. Here we see the power of the poet in describing home-life, in depicting character; and here, too, we see the moralist and philosopher.

Whittier was first of all a teacher; to him duty was august, her commands imperative. This did not please the *dilettanti*. It has always offended those who fail to see the highest and divinest mission in art. The teacher, the philosopher, the moralist—these must be sneered down. They are disquieting; they compel us to think; they startle our conscience; they compel us to boldly take sides in the great battle of progress which is being waged, or win the contempt of our better selves. It is not pleasant to break with conventionalism, it is also perilous to do so; let us remain as we are; let us parley with wrong if we cannot ignore it, but do not compel us to join the maligned and slandered minority. Such is the voice of conventionalism. But the true prophet cannot heed the smooth tongue of the charmer. He has a mission; God's hand has touched his eyes; he sees the enormity of the injustice on every hand; he beholds the splendid possibilities which lie beyond humanity's conquest of animality or selfism. He cannot remain silent; he cannot prophesy pleasant things. He is an optimist, and therefore he refuses to allow the hideous wrongs to fester when health and happiness lie within the grasp of humanity the moment shortsighted selfishness is exchanged for wisdom. Whittier was always a teacher, always a moralist. If in the later years he came to some extent under the spell of conventionalism and ceased to be the aggressive reformer he had been in early manhood, he never ceased to be a teacher.

Here is one of those rare glimpses (embalmed) in descriptive verse which reveal the artist power in the poet and which constitute one of the chief charms of many of Whittier's pictures of life in New England. As the reader will quickly recognize, it is taken from "Snow-Bound":

> As night drew on and, from the crest
> Of wooded knolls that ridged the west,
> The sun, a snow-blown traveller, sank
> From sight beneath the smothering bank.

We piled, with care, our nightly stack
Of wood against the chimney back,—
The oaken log, green, huge and thick,
And on its top the stout back-stick ;
The knotty forestick laid apart,
And filled between with curious art
The ragged brush ; then, hovering near,
We watched the first red blaze appear,
Heard the sharp crackle, caught the gleam
On whitewashed wall and sagging beam,
Until the old, rude-furnished room
Burst, flower-like, into rosy bloom.

*   *   *   *   *

Shut in from all the world without,
We sat the clean-winged hearth about,
Content to let the north-wind roar
In baffled rage at pane and door,
While the red logs before us beat
The frost-line back with tropic heat ;
And ever, when a louder blast
Shook beam and rafter as it passed,
The merrier up its roaring draught
The great throat of the chimney laughed,
The house-dog on his paws outspread
Laid to the fire his drowsy head.

Next we find the reminiscent poet becoming the moralizer, as was his wont, and the
great problem of the future, ever present

when he gave himself up to serious musing, challenges his attention, as it does more than once in subsequent lines of the same poem :

What matter how the night behaved ?
What matter how the north-wind raved ?
Blow high, blow low, not all its snow
Could quench our hearth-fire's ruddy glow.
O Time and Change!—with hair as gray
As was my sire's that winter day,
How strange it seems, with so much gone
Of life and love, to still live on !
Ah, brother! only I and thou
Are left of all that circle now,—
The dear home faces whereupon
That fitful firelight paled and shone.
Henceforward, listen as we will,
The voices of that hearth are still;
Look where we may, the wide world o'er,
Those lighted faces smile no more.

    *   *   *   *   *

Yet Love will dream, and Faith will trust,
(Since He who knows our need is just),
That somehow, somewhere, meet we must.
Alas for him who never sees
The stars shine through his cypress trees!
Who, hopeless, lays his dead away,
Nor looks to see the breaking day
Across the mournful marbles play!

24

Who hath not learned, in hours of faith,
  The truth to flesh and sense unknown,
That Life is ever lord of Death,
  And Love can never lose its own!

We come very near to the heart of that memorable little circle, as we read these lines in which some members of the group are described in Whittier's frank, graphic and simple manner :

We sped the time with stories old,
Wrought puzzles out, and riddles told.

*   *   *   *   *

Our mother, while she turned her wheel
Or run the new-knit stocking-heel,
Told how the Indian hordes came down
At midnight on Cochecho town,
And how her own great-uncle bore
His cruel scalp-mark to fourscore.
Recalling, in her fitting phrase,
  So rich and picturesque and free
  (The common unrhymed poetry
Of simple life and country ways),
The story of her early days,—
She made us welcome to her home;
Old hearths grew wide to give us room;

We stole with her a frightened look
At the gray wizard's conjuring-book,
The fame whereof went far and wide
Through all the simple country side;
We heard the hawks at twilight play,
The boat-horn on Piscataqua,
The loon's weird laughter far away.

*   *   *   *   *

Our uncle, innocent of books,
Was rich in lore of fields and brooks,
The ancient teachers never dumb
Of Nature's unhoused lyceum.
In moons and tides and weather wise,
He read the clouds as prophecies,
And foul or fair could well divine,
By many an occult hint and sign,
Holding the cunning-warded keys
To all the woodcraft mysteries ;
Himself to Nature's heart so near
That all her voices in his ear
Of beast or bird had meanings clear,
Like Apollonius of old,
Who knew the tales the sparrows told,
Or Hermes, who interpreted
What the sage cranes of Nilus said ;
A simple, guileless, childlike man,
Content to live where life began.

*   *   *   *   *

Next, the dear aunt, whose smile of cheer
And voice in dreams I see and hear,—
The sweetest woman ever Fate
Perverse denied a household mate,
Who, lonely, homeless, not the less
Found peace in love's unselfishness,
And welcome wheresoe'er she went,
A calm and gracious element,
Whose presence seemed the sweet income
And womanly atmosphere of home,—
Called up her girlhood memories,
The huskings and the apple-bees,
The sleigh rides and the summer sails,
Weaving through all the poor details
And homespun warp of circumstance
A golden woof-thread of romance.

*   *   *   *   *

Through years of toil and soil and care,
From glossy tress to thin gray hair,
All unprofaned she held apart
The virgin fancies of the heart.

*   *   *   *   *

There, too, our elder sister plied
Her evening task the stand beside ;   .
A full, rich nature, free to trust,
Truthful and almost sternly just,
Impulsive, earnest, prompt to act,
And make her generous thought a fact,

27

Keeping with many a light disguise
The secret of self-sacrifice.
O heart sore-tried ! thou hast the best
That heaven itself could give thee,—*rest.*

*   *   *   *   *

As one who held herself a part
Of all she saw, and let her heart
  Against the household bosom lean,
Upon the motley-braided mat
Our youngest and our dearest sat,
Lifting her large, sweet, asking eyes,
  Now bathed within the fadeless green
And holy peace of Paradise.

*   *   *   *   *

With me one little year ago :—
The chill weight of the winter snow
  For months upon her grave has lain ;
And now, when summer south-winds blow
  And briar and harebell bloom again,
I tread the pleasant paths we trod,
I see the violet-sprinkled sod
Whereon she leaned, too frail and weak
The hillside flowers she loved to seek,
Yet following me where'er I went
With dark eyes full of love's content.

*   *   *   *   *

28

I cannot feel that thou art far,
Since near at need the angels are ;
And when the sunset gates unbar,
   Shall I not see thee waiting stand,
And, white against the evening star,
   The welcome of thy beckoning hand ?

An incident in the life of the aunt referred to above was frequently related by Whittier when talking over psychical and spiritual matters with friends greatly interested in such subjects. The main points in this story, which is interesting alike to students of psychical phenomena and to lovers of romance, are as follows :

The poet's aunt was betrothed to a young man who was absent in the state of New York. One winter evening the Quaker maiden had lingered over the great wood fire in the spacious kitchen until the others had retired. At length she rose and, turning to the window, beheld without in the clear moonlight which fell on a landscape wrapped in snow her lover approaching on horseback. She hastened to the door, noticing as she passed the window that he had reined in his horse as if to leap from the saddle. On opening the door, however, no one was visible. Then a great fear fell upon her, which grew into a nameless terror; she called her sister, and related the strange vision, and expressed her forebodings. In vain did the sympathetic sister try to reason away her apprehensions, suggesting that she had been dreaming; the maiden only shook her head, affirming that she had never been more thoroughly awake. Some days later a letter came to her written by a stranger telling of the death of her lover at the very time when she had beheld his apparition.

To his mother, lovingly described in " Snow-Bound," Whittier owed more than to any other person for his success as a poet. While the father, a plain, prosaic and matter-of-fact man, frowned upon his verse-making and discouraged him, the mother lent him sympathy and encouragement. She also stored his mind with legends and stories which later he immortalized in his simple and heart-reaching lays. This mother was a very superior woman, and the moulding power which she exerted over her son cannot be overestimated. Her influence, and the poetry of Burns, were far more to the poet than the benefits he received from the district school, or the academy at which he spent a short time. Burns was a real educator to Whittier; the Scottish bard fulfilled the function of a true teacher in calling out or developing the latent power in the poet's mind, and teaching him how to appreciate the beauty in the commonplace things of life. He was fourteen years old when a copy of the Scotch poet's works fell into his hands. In his autobiographical notes Whittier thus refers to his introduction to Burns:

"When I was fourteen years old, my first schoolmaster, Joshua Coffin, the able, eccentric historian of Newbury, brought with him to our house a volume of Burns' poems, from which he read, greatly to my delight. I begged him to leave the book with me, and set myself at once to the task of mastering the glossary of the Scottish dialect at its close. This was about the first poetry I ever read—with the exception of that of the Bible, of which I had been a close student—and it had a lasting influence upon me. I began to make rhymes myself, and to imagine stories and adventures. In fact, I lived a sort of dual life, and in a world of fancy as well as in the world of plain matter of fact about me."

Robert Collyer, in relating a conversation which he had with the poet, quotes Whittier as follows:

"Burns is to me the noblest poet of our

race. He was the first poet I read, and he will be the last. . . . I read Burns every moment I had to spare. And this was one great result to me of my communion with him: I found that the things out of which poems came were not, as I had always imagined, somewhere away off in a world and life lying outside the edge of our own New England sky—they were right here about my feet and among the people I knew. The common things of our common life I found were full of poetry."

It is the true teacher who so instructs the childish mind that it learns to apprehend the beauties and truths which lie around it, who stimulates the imagination and awakens the noble sentiments of the soul, who succeeds in calling into independent action the reasoning faculties, and centres the youthful thought upon the vital problems of life as they affect the peace, happiness and elevation of man.

Whittier inherited a deeply poetic nature; his imagination was limited, but within its bounds it was compelling in its power. He also inherited a deeply spiritual nature. On one occasion, when in conversation with a friend, he described a sense of awe and almost oppressive solemnity which suddenly came over him one evening as he was driving home the cows—he was only seven years of age—when the thought, " Why am I different from those cows, what have I got to do in life, what is life ? " swept in upon his startled mind.*

" He never lost the impression of that hour," observed his friend. " It affected his whole life."

He was a born dreamer. In reply to a little girl who wrote him of his childhood, he said: " I think at the age of which thy note inquires, I found about equal satisfaction in an old rural home with the shifting

* " Whittier with the Children." By Margaret Sidney.

panorama of seasons, in reading the few books within my reach, and in dreaming of something wonderful and grand in the future." In reminiscent moods the poet often related how, when a boy, his imagination carried him far away from the work in hand and, lost in dreams, he would lean upon his hoe or spade until his father, "a prompt, decisive man," would call out, "That's enough for a stand, John."

The work on the farm was ill suited to one so delicate as Whittier and, when seventeen years of age, he sustained from overexertion injuries from which he never recovered. Yet this apparent calamity was not an unmixed evil, as it helped to gain for him his father's consent to his going to the Haverhill Academy. Heretofore, the only regular schooling the poet had enjoyed had been received in the district schools, which were very indifferent in character. He had written many verses which his sister Mary had highly complimented. One day this sister, who had always occupied a very large place in the poet's heart, sent one of his poems to Garrison for the Newbury *Free Press*. The poet knew nothing of the submitting of the lines, and the editor was ignorant of the authorship. However, on reading them Mr. Garrison promptly published the poem. Whittier was spellbound when he found his stanzas in print. In referring to this experience Mr. Pickard observes:

" His heart stood still a moment. Such delight as his comes only once in the lifetime of any aspirant to literary fame. His father at last called to him to put up the paper and continue his work, but he could not resist the temptation to take the paper again and again from his pocket to stare at his lines in print. He has said he was sure he did not read a word of the poem all the time he looked at it."

Garrison found out by inquiry who the youthful poet was, and forthwith drove out to the Whittier homestead to meet the young author. On the editor inquiring of the father for his son John, the worthy Quaker became much agitated, fearing that his boy had in some way got into trouble or disgrace ; when, however, the facts were made known, the old gentleman was much relieved, but he frowned upon Garrison's suggestion that the boy be encouraged in his literary aspirations. " Poetry will not bring him bread," exclaimed the old man—a fact which Garrison could not then gainsay.

The visit, however, fanned anew the ambition of the dreamer boy. He importuned his father to let him go to the academy about to be opened in Haverhill. At length it was agreed that if Whittier could earn sufficient money by working nights to pay his way he might go. The youth made shoes during the winter evenings and thus earned enough for his first six months at the academy. Subsequently he taught school for a short time and assisted in posting books, and in this manner earned enough for his second term.

Thus, with the slight profit derived from the district school and two terms at the academy, Whittier went forth to play upon the heartstrings of his fellow-men and touch the conscience of a nation in a manner seldom equalled in this century. He entered upon the aggressive warfare that marked his early manhood without the polish which lent grace to the work of several of his contemporaries; but he also escaped the paralyzing influence of soulless conventionalism, whose skeleton fingers extend from a dead past, and too often crush originality and throttle the voice of conscience in aspiring youths, while they are pursuing the curriculum of our conservative educational institutions. If he lacked in polish, he possessed what were of far more importance —a heart aflame with love of justice, a nature pure and simple, and a brain stored with "knowledge never learned in books and schools." His boyhood days, if uneventful, were far from uninteresting; and the pictures he has given us of old New England life, no less than the hopes, joys and sorrows which filled the horizon of his boyish world, are dear to our people, and will continue to be a source of pleasure and inspiration for many generations to come.

Ah! thou little barefoot dreamer boy, who wanderedst over the hills and vales round thy native home, revelling in the beauty and fragrance of our wild flora, charmed by the matchless music of the forest's feathered orchestra, awed by the sublimity of Nature in her grander manifestations, thou child of pure and honest parents, had we more lives like thine, the curses of our day and generation would lose their power, and in the place of feverish hate, misery, poverty, drunkenness, debauchery, bigotry, intolerance and woe, we should see peace, love, prosperity, purity and nobility open their blossoms on every side ; earth would put on Eden-like beauty ; and humanity, with great strides, would sweep onward and upward toward the sun-bathed plane of perfect civilization. And all peoples, even as the voice of one man, could unite in these words from thy song of triumph :

> The airs of heaven blow o'er me;
> A glory shines before me
> Of what mankind shall be,—
> Pure, generous, brave, and free.
>
> A dream of man and woman
> Diviner but still human,
> Solving the riddle old,
> Shaping the Age of Gold.
>
> The love of God and neighbor;
> An equal-handed labor ;
> The richer life, where beauty
> Walks hand in hand with duty.

*   *   *   *

I feel the earth move sunward,
I join the great march onward,
And take, by faith, while living,
My freehold of thanksgiving.

A PROPHET OF FREEDOM.

"O Freedom ! if to me belong
Nor mighty Milton's gift divine,
        Nor Marvell's wit and graceful song ;
        Still with a love as deep and strong
As theirs I lay, like them, my best gifts on thy shrine !"
                                        —*Whittier.*

"Or should he deem wrong there at the public weal,
    Lo ! the whole man seemed girt with flashing steel,
    His glance a sword-thrust, and his words of fire
    Like thunder tones from some old prophet's lyre."
                                        —*Hayne.*

"We already see—and the future will see it more clearly
—that no party ever did a vaster work than his party ; that
he, like Hampden and Milton, is a character not produced
in common times."
                                        —*E. C. Stedman.*

II. A Prophet of Freedom.

IN the history of many an individual,
especially among those who have
left their impress on their age,
there comes a time when the trend of the
life seems to turn on the most insignificant
happening. This apparently destiny-shap-
ing event or decision does not, of course,
change the character of the individual, making him good or bad when before he had
been the opposite, although it may greatly
strengthen and develop good or bad char-
acteristics previously existing in his nature.
It must be borne in mind that behind the
momentous though seemingly unimportant
occurrence, is the individual's personality
with its dower of qualities received through
the complex and interblended influences of

heredity, and prenatal and postnatal conditions. There is the brain with its potential grasp, its imagination, and the marvellous alchemic power by which ideas are transmuted into living agencies capable of influencing other minds, and shaping the destiny of nations and of civilizations. There is the conscience, awake, or asleep but present,—there is the soul, awaiting the moving of the waters by the spirit of God. But this trivial something, which is yet so influential if not so absolutely destiny-fixing in character, acts as a branch which, falling from a tree, changes the course of a river near its source, so that it flows into the ocean hundreds of miles from where it would have entered the sea had nothing deflected its current. Does anything *happen* in our world? Have the " ifs " of history any real place in serious contemplation? Is man a creature of free will, or of destiny? or do both these agencies act and react upon each other?

I incline to think the last view correct. But the fact that the most momentous events in the history of humanity seem frequently to have hung on the most trivial occurrences, often the feeble will of a fragile child (as, for example, in the case of the Maid of Orleans), affords a most interesting subject for speculation. And so with the lives of many who have powerfully influenced the brain and conscience of their fellow-men; frequently, it seems that the current of their destiny has veered at the whim apparently of trifles.

In the life of Whittier we find one of these momentous but seemingly insignificant incidents,—the sister secretly sends her brother's poem to William Lloyd Garrison, whose first impulse is to destroy without reading it. The young editor, however, is impelled to glance over the creation and is impressed with its power. He publishes it, and forthwith seeks to ascertain the name of the author; after succeeding, he visits the Whittier homestead and urges the father to look favorably on the suggestion of his son being allowed to secure a better education. This visit exerts a most pronounced effect upon the youthful poet. It fans to flame his ambition, leading him to make one of those all-compelling resolutions that brook no failure. He succeeds in entering the academy, and is subsequently launched upon a literary career, editing three different journals during 1828 and 1833.*

For five years after entering public life Whittier practically refrained from casting in his lot with the despised band of Abolitionists, who were then the recipients of all the epithets of abuse which unreasoning prejudice and easy-going conventionalism always employ so prodigally when seeking to clothe with ignominy those who insist on

* The *American Manufacturer*, the *Haverhill Gazette*, and *The New England Review*.

arousing the sleeping conscience of society by demanding a higher regard for the demands of justice and morality. The facts involved seem to clearly indicate that it was Garrison's influence which at last turned the scales leading Whittier, after his five years of waiting, to boldly embrace the cause of Abolition. Not that his sympathies had at any time been elsewhere than with the cause of freedom, but he was a Quaker; he loved peace and his intuitive mind quickly perceived, what many less far-seeing men failed to appreciate, that the onward movement of the Abolition cause meant riots, mobs and bloodshed,—perhaps, it meant war and the severance of the Union. He hoped to see the cause triumph peaceably, even if so it should be longer in the process of settlement. Then again he had political and literary ambitions which he well knew would be blasted if he espoused the unpopular cause. He shrank from the contempt of his fellow-men, and he dreaded the savage conflict which he felt would follow an aggressive campaign for unconditional abolition. He cherished as long as possible the hope that justice would triumph over greed; but the time came when he could not answer Garrison's arguments to his own satisfaction, for he could not close his eyes to the fact that the trend of politics, and the commercial demands and requirements of the time, were distinctly opposed to his own vision of gradual emancipation. In order to win electoral votes from the South, the two great parties throughout the North were vying with each other in disciplining those members who pleaded for freedom and justice to all men. The cotton gin and the increase of rice culture made the dream of gradual emancipation thoroughly visionary; at least it seemed so to Whittier, who had carefully studied the question with an earnest desire to be convinced that the theory of gradual emancipation was probable, if the facts at all warranted such a conclusion. His hope, however, grew less and less the more he considered the question. Garrison, who through his early friendship with the poet was able to approach nearer to his conscience than anyone else, brought all his influence to bear upon the young Quaker to convince him of his duty, and to outweigh Whittier's natural reluctance to engaging in aggressive warfare, his supersensitiveness, and his ambition for political honors.

In 1833, Whittier crossed the Rubicon by publishing at his own expense a carefully prepared argument on "Justice and Expediency." This done, he found himself forced into the heart of the band who were struggling for an interpretation of freedom wider than the nation had yet recognized. His poem inscribed to Garrison * reveals his

* According to Mr. Pickard, this poem was published in the *Haverhill Gazette* in November, 1831 ; while Mr. Wil-

strong attachment to the friend of his youth, and his admiration for the moral courage of the foremost apostle of Abolition, as will be seen from these stanzas :

Champion of those who groan beneath
  Oppression's iron hand :
In view of penury, hate, and death,
  I see thee fearless stand,
Still bearing up thy lofty brow,
  In the steadfast strength of truth,
In manhood sealing well the vow
  And promise of thy youth.

      *   *   *   *

I love thee with a brother's love,
  I feel my pulses thrill,
To mark thy spirit soar above
  The cloud of human ill.
My heart hath leaped to answer thine,
  And echo back thy words,

---

liam Sloane Kennedy, in his " Life of Whittier," maintains that it was not published until after " Justice and Expediency." If Mr. Pickard is correct, it indicates that the strong attachment of the poet for Garrison, and his admiration for the man who was being so generally maligned, led to this outburst of feeling, in verse which reflected the sentiments of the youthful editor who was not yet ready to cast in his lines with Garrison.

As leaps the warrior's at the shine
  And flash of kindred swords!

*　　*　　*　　*

Have I not known thee well, and read
  Thy mighty purpose long ?
And watched the trials which have made
  Thy human spirit strong ?
And shall the slanderer's demon breath
  Avail with one like me,
To dim the sunshine of my faith
  And earnest trust in thee ?

In taking his stand Whittier made one of
those sublime sacrifices which evince the essential divinity immanent in man.　For even
those who do not sympathize with his decision, deeming the action to have been
unwise, unless they be blinded by unreasoning prejudice will appreciate the grandeur
of soul which led an ambitious young man
with the most flattering political and literary
prospects before him to turn his back upon
honor, success, and the natural inclinations
of his nature, and consent to be a social

outcast for the cause his conscience approved. No one, be it remembered, was better acquainted with the nature of the sacrifice he was making than the poet; he had carefully surveyed the whole field from the position of one whose opportunities enabled him to comprehend the magnitude of the sacrifice. On this point, Mr. William Sloane Kennedy observes:

"When Whittier espoused the cause of the slave he had counted the cost, and knew that he was burying all hope of political preferment and literary gains. Those who gave themselves to the work knew not but that it might be for a lifetime. To be shunned and spat upon by society, mobbed in public, and injured in one's business,—this was what it meant to become an Abolitionist. When Miss Martineau avowed her sympathy with them, society shut its doors in her face. When Longfellow put forth his little pamphlet of poems on slavery, weak and harmless as they were, the editor of *Graham's Magazine* wrote him to offer excuses for the brevity of a guarded notice of the poems, saying that the word 'slavery' was never allowed to appear in a Philadelphia periodical, and that the publisher of the magazine had objected to have even the name of the book appear in his pages. Allusion only can be made to a few of the innumerable persecutions endured by the friends of the black race. How Lydia Maria Child was deprived of the use of the Athenæum Library, in Boston, because the first use she had made of it was to prepare her 'appeal'; how Dr. Follen was deprived of his professorship in Harvard College for his brave espousal of Abolitionism; how Prudence Crandall's schoolhouse was defiled with filth, and its windows broken; how Arthur Tappan's house was sacked and his life threatened; how Dr. Reuben Crandall (teacher of botany in Washington, D. C., and brother of Prudence Crandall) for having, at his own request, lent to a white citizen a copy of Whittier's ' Justice and Expediency ' was kept in a damp city prison for eight months, until the seeds of consumption were sown, and his life made a sacrifice ; how Amos Dresser was flogged in the public square of Nashville, and his fellow-student of Lane Seminary, the eloquent Marius R. Robinson, was dragged from his bed at night, and tarred and feathered by ruffians,—all these things are matters of history."

This noble sacrifice of the lower to the higher afforded the poet the keenest pleasure throughout life, as such soul-victories always afford high-minded, sincere natures ; and he attributed his later success largely to this momentous decision. Toward the close of his life he said as much to a youth of fifteen years who sought his counsel, adding, " Join thyself to some unpopular but noble cause, if thou wouldst succeed." The poet had in mind, without doubt, the only success which is worthy of the name,—success from which flows the triumph of right and the enlargement of human happiness.

The years 1834 and 1835 are known as the "mob" years of the anti-slavery educational period. In New York, disturbances were of frequent occurrence ; but the spirit of lawlessness on the part of conventional society which plumed itself on being ultra-respectable was also present in various other centres. It was on the twenty-first of October, 1835, that Garrison was mobbed by the so-called "respectables" of Boston. In writing of this outrage, Miss Martineau observes that an eminent Boston lawyer said to her : "Oh ! there was no mob ; I was there myself, and saw that they were all gentlemen,—they were all in fine broadcloth. * * * They only wanted to show him that they would not have such a person live amongst them."

It is interesting to remember here that it was this mobbing of Garrison that served to sweep Wendell Phillips into the ranks of the Abolitionists.

In 1835 the poet and his friend, George Thompson (an Englishman, afterwards a member of Parliament), were mobbed in Concord, New Hampshire. The experience was quite thrilling. The poet, who had ventured forth for a stroll, was set upon by a crowd of people who, by imbibing freely of strong drink, had fortified themselves for the arduous task of preventing free speech. At first, only oaths and vile language were hurled at the poet; but mobs are nothing if not intemperate, and soon mud, gravel and stones were showered upon the young man, who was beating a hasty retreat—before he could reach a place of refuge, he had lost his hat and had received a rather severe stone-bruise on his cheek. The disorderly throng constantly grew in size and became more violent and lawless as night came on. Finally they gathered before the home of the host of the two Abolitionists and demanded Whittier and Thompson, declaring that if they were not delivered up to them they would blow up the place. The inmates of the house, however, were no cowards, nor did they lose their presence of mind; after a hasty council, it was decided to hitch up the carriage and, if possible, divert the attention of the rapidly increasing crowd, until the visitors could get beyond the danger line. The plan succeeded. The attention of the mob was cleverly diverted, while the door of the carriage house was opened and the horses plunged forward at a gallop, carrying Whittier and Thompson beyond the reach of danger.

Many years later the poet chanced to be in Portland, Maine, where he was accosted by a gentleman who inquired whether he was not the poet Whittier; on receiving an affirmative answer, the gentleman in question informed the poet that he had been in the mob and, he continued, he believed a devil possessed him that night, for he had no prejudice to satisfy or desire to harm either Whittier or Thompson, but coming within the influence of the mob he was seized by an intense desire to kill them, and believed he should have done so had they not escaped. He stated that the mob was like a company of demons, and he knew one man who had mixed to dip the fugitives in a dye, which its maker assured him would have proved well-nigh indelible. "I have never been able," concluded this man, "to account in a manner satisfactory to myself for the strange mental condition I was in that night." This confession is interesting to students of psychology; it illustrates the strong psychological influence which some minds come under when exposed to the thought waves generated by a gathering in which intense passion has drowned reason, and men and women have ceased to be the creatures of aught else than prejudice and brutal desire.

The meetings of the Abolitionists were frequently broken up by turbulent bands, even when no violence was shown, and many are the ludicrous incidents which occurred at these gatherings. On one occasion, a lady who was accustomed to give the friends of freedom no end of trouble by her continual interruptions and who, being possessed of some wit, usually created great amusement among the unsympathetic onlookers who frequented these assemblies, became so troublesome that in order to continue the meeting it was necessary to remove the loquacious disturber. Finally, Wendell Phillips and two other gentlemen gently raised her chair and proceeded to carry her from the hall; she was by no means disconcerted but, in fact, seemed to enjoy the situation. The trio had not proceeded far, however, when she broke the silence by exclaiming: "I am better off than my Master was, for He had but one ass to ride on, while I have three to carry me." Whittier used to relate another amusing incident that occurred about this time: One of the public meetings became very stormy, more on account of the opposing views entertained by the friends of freedom than from the disorderly class who usually gave trouble. Now, there were seated on the platform William Lloyd Garrison, whose head was very bald; William A. Burleigh, whose hair fell in a great mane on his shoulders; and a negro. Suddenly, during a momentary lull, some one in the rear of the hall shouted: "Mr. Speaker, Mr. Speaker, I have only a word to say. If that negro will shave Burleigh and make a whig for Garrison all difference will be settled." The house instantly broke forth in roars of laughter which lasted for some time and seemed to put every one in a good humor, as from that moment the meeting passed off smoothly, a rare good humor seeming to have taken the place of the almost bitter spirit which had prevailed a few moments before.

In 1838 the beautiful temple of freedom in Philadelphia dedicated as Pennsylvania Hall was burned by a mob. This act of lawlessness created a deep impression on many thoughtful minds throughout the North. In his editorial in the issue of the *Pennsylvania Tribune* which appeared after the burning, Whittier speaks in these vivid, vital and prophetic sentences of the outrage and the influence which it would exert upon the friends of freedom: "Not in vain, we trust, has the persecution fallen upon us. Fresher and purer for the fiery baptism, the cause lives in our hearts. * * * Woe unto us if we

falter through the fear of man !   *   *   *
Citizens of Pennsylvania ! your rights as well
as ours have been violated in this dreadful
outrage.   *   *   *   In the heart of your
free city, within view of the Hall of Inde-
pendence, whose spire and roof reddened in
the flame of the sacrifice, the deed has been
done,—and the shout which greeted the falling ruin was the shout of Slavery over the
grave of Liberty.   *   *   *   Are we pointed
to the smoking ruins of that beautiful
Temple of Freedom, which we fondly hoped
would have long echoed the noble and free
sentiments of a Franklin, a Rush, a Benezet,
a Jay; and as we look sadly on its early
downfall, are we bidden to learn hence the
fate of our own dwellings if we persevere?
Think not the intimidation will drive us from
our post.   *   *   *   We feel that God has
called us to this work, and if it be His purpose that we should finish what we have be-
gun, He can preserve us, though it be as in

the lion's den, or the seven-fold heated furnace."

Whittier's poems during this period were thrown off at white heat. In later life he thus characterized them: " Of their defects from an artistic point of view it is not necessary to speak. They were the earnest and often vehement expression of the writer's thought and feeling at critical periods in the great conflict between Freedom and Slavery. They were written with no expectation that they would survive the occasions which called them forth; they were protests, alarm signals, trumpet calls to action, words wrung from the writer's heart, forged at white heat, and of course lacking the finish and careful word-selection which reflection and patient brooding over them might have given." They were indeed trumpet calls, and did more to awaken the sleeping conscience of the nation than even our historians appreciate. James Russell Lowell was profoundly impressed, and generously expressed his appreciation of Whittier in these striking lines: "Whittier has always been found faithful to the Muses' holy trust. He has not put his talent out at profitable interest, by catering to the insolent and Pharisaical self-esteem of the times; nor has he hidden it in the damask napkin of historical commonplaces, or a philanthropy too universal to concern itself with particular wrongs, the practical redressing of which is all that renders philanthropy of value. Most poets are content to follow the spirit of their age, as pigeons follow a leaky grain-cart, picking a kernel here and there out of the dry dust of the past. Not so with Whittier. From the heart of the onset upon the serried mercenaries of every tyranny, the chords of his iron-strung lyre clang with a martial and triumphant cheer; and where Freedom's Spartan few maintain their inviolate mountain pass against the assaults of Slavery, his voice may be heard, clear and fearless, as if the victory were already won. It is with the highest satisfaction I send you the enclosed poem, every way worthy of our truly New England poet." And Thomas Wentworth Higginson, in a tribute to Whittier written some years since, thus expresses the wonderful influence exerted by the poet over his youthful imagination :

At dawn of manhood came a voice to me
   That said to the startled conscience, "Sleep no more !"

     *   *   *   *   *   *   *

If any good to me or from me came,
   Through life, and if no influence less divine
Has quite usurped the place of duty's flame ;
   If aught rose worthy in this heart of mine,
Aught that, viewed backward, wears no shade of shame ;
   Bless thee, old friend! for that high call was thine.

This brings us to notice some of Whittier's poems relating to the anti-slavery struggle. It cannot be expected that these stanzas will thrill or influence us as they did the Northern mind during the exciting days when they were written, any more than the picture of an army rushing to glory and savage death can awaken the horror and sense of anguish that the actual battle would inspire. But on the other hand we at the present time, and especially those of us who have grown up since the terrible civil strife, can view these creations with eyes less blinded by partiality or prejudice than would have been possible if we had attempted to estimate this phase of Whittier's life at an earlier day. We who have grown to manhood and womanhood since the close of the civil war shall be able to appreciate the high motives, the sincerity and superb power of the poet, even though the sympathies of some of us may run counter to his thought. We are furthermore able to accord him a degree of justice which it would not have been reasonable, perhaps, for us to expect those of an older generation to have shown; for we appreciate the fact that he necessarily viewed the question of slavery from a point of view which prevented his gaining more than a partial grasp of the situation, and which prevented his knowing of the brighter aspects of plantation life, no less than of the difficulties and perplexities which the Southerners had to grapple with—about which, indeed, none of the Abolitionists knew much.

Having thus reached a point sufficiently removed from the conflict to enable us to justly judge and impartially view the work of the poet, whether we agree with him or dissent from his view, we pass to the notice of the poems more as the outgushing of a prophetic soul that conscientiously sought to awaken the sleeping conscience of the people ; and in this judicial attitude we shall notice his creations apart from their partizan bearing, or even their specific relation to the slavery question, as by maintaining this mental posture we can consider Whittier's character as a typical reformer more fairly than would be possible if our views were colored by passion or prejudice.

In the following lines the poet-seer strives, through an appeal to reason, patriotism, manhood, and man's innate sense of justice, to avert the gloom and horror of war, and the degradation which he felt a nation must sink into which continued to be guilty of slavery after the conscience had been called to judgment :

> Up, then, in Freedom's manly part,
>   From graybeard eld to fiery youth,
> And on the nation's naked heart
>   Scatter the living coals of truth !
> Up,—while ye slumber, deeper yet
>   The shadow of our shame is growing !
> Up,—while ye pause, our sun may set
>   In blood, around our altars flowing !
>
> Oh ! rouse ye, ere the storm comes forth,—
>   The gathered wrath of God and man,—
> Like that which wasted Egypt's earth,
>   When hail and fire above it ran.
> Hear ye no warnings in the air ?
>   Feel ye no earthquake underneath ?
> Up,—*up !* Why will ye slumber where
>   The sleeper only wakes in death ?

Up now for freedom !—not in strife
  Like that your sterner fathers saw,—
The awful waste of human life,—
  The glory and the guilt of war :
But break the chain,—the yoke remove,
  And smite to earth Oppression's rod,
With those mild arms of Truth and Love,
  Made mighty through the living God !

I always think of Jesus in the Temple driving out the money changers, overturning the tables and crying in austere tones, "It is written my house shall be called a house of prayer, but ye have made it a den of thieves," when I read the following verses, which are taken from a poem entitled "Clerical Oppressors," called forth by the celebrated pro-slavery meeting in Charleston, S. C., Sept. 4, 1835. To quote from the *Courier* of that city, "The clergy of all denominations attended in a body, lending their sanction to the proceedings, and adding by their presence to the impressive character of the scene." When Whittier read these lines a feeling of amazement gave place to one of horror and indignation, as from his lips leaped forth such words as the following:

Just God !—and these are they
   Who minister at thine altar, God of Right !
Men who their hands with prayer and blessing lay
   On Israel's Ark of light !

What ! servants of thy own
   Merciful Son, who came to seek and save
The homeless and the outcast,—fettering down
   The tasked and plundered slave !

Paid hypocrites, who turn
   Judgment aside, and rob the Holy Book
Of those high words of truth which search and burn
   In warning and rebuke ;

Feed fat, ye locusts, feed!
   And in your tasselled pulpits, thank the Lord
That, from the toiling bondman's utter need,
   Ye pile your own full board.

How long, O Lord ! how long
   Shall such a priesthood barter truth away,
And in thy name, for robbery and wrong
   At thy own altars pray ?

Woe, then, to all who grind
  Their brethren of a common Father down !
To all who plunder from the immortal mind
  Its bright and glorious crown!

O, speed the moment on
  When Wrong shall cease, and Liberty and Love
And Truth and Right throughout the earth be known
  As in their home above.

These stanzas are unlike Whittier,—as was Jesus' action in the Temple unlike the general course pursued by that one of whom it was written, "A bruised reed will he not break, or smoking flax will he not quench;" and they indicate, no less vividly than did the action of the great Nazarene, how profoundly the sense of shame and indignation was stirred in the poet at the spectacle of the entire clergy of an opulent city lending sanction to the institution of slavery.

The poem entitled, "Massachusetts to Virginia," created a profound impression and was quoted at length throughout the North. The rugged spirit of freedom and the love of justice which characterized the sturdy Saxon people of olden time are very marked in these lines from this notable poem :

We hear thy threats, Virginia ! thy stormy words and high
Swell harshly on the southern winds which melt along our
    sky ;
Yet, not one brown, hard hand foregoes its honest labor
    here,—
No hewer of our mountain oaks suspends his axe in fear.

Wild are the waves which lash the reefs along St. George's
    bank,—
Cold on the shore of Labrador the fog lies white and dank ;
Through storm and wave and blinding mist stout are the
    hearts which man
The fishing-smacks of Marblehead, the sea-boats of Cape
    Ann.

The cold north light and wintry sun glare on their icy
    forms,
Bent grimly o'er their straining lines or wrestling with the
    storms ;
Free as the winds they drive before, rough as the waves
    they roam,
They laugh to scorn the slaver's threat against their rocky
    home.

What means the Old Dominion ?   Hath she forgot the day
When o'er her conquered valleys swept the Briton's steel
    array ?
How side by side, with sons of hers, the Massachusetts men
Encountered Tarleton's charge of fire, and stout Cornwallis,
    then ?

Forgets she how the Bay State, in answer to the call
Of her old House of Burgesses, spoke out from Faneuil
    Hall ?
When, echoing back her Henry's cry, came pulsing on each
    breath
Of Northern winds, the thrilling sounds of " LIBERTY OR
    DEATH !"

  *   *   *   *   *

All that a *sister* State should do, all that a *free* State may,
Heart, hand, and purse we proffer, as in our early day ;
But that one dark loathsome burden ye must stagger with
    alone,
And reap the bitter harvest which ye yourselves have
    sown !

Hold, while ye may, your struggling slaves, and burden
    God's free air
With woman's shriek beneath the lash, and manhood's wild
    despair ;
Cling closer to the " cleaving curse " that writes upon your
    plains
The blasting of Almighty wrath against a land of chains.

  *   *   *   *   *

We wage no war,—we lift no arm,—we fling no torch within
The fire-damps of the quaking mine beneath your soil of sin ;
We leave ye with your bondmen, to wrestle, while ye can,
With the strong upward tendencies and godlike soul of man !

But for us and for our children, the vow which we have given
For freedom and humanity is registered in heaven ;
No slave-hunt in our borders,—no pirate on our strand !
No fetters in the Bay State,—no slave upon our land !

The spirit which throbs through the above stanzas is the spirit of justice, of progress, and the dawn; and whether we are ready to see as Whittier saw or not, we must recognize the eternal soul of Right as pulsing through the lines. And these verses from " Texas," although they are not exactly what one would expect from a Quaker, the spirit being distinctly defiant, yet they must have been electrifying in their effect upon the aroused conscience of men and women who were so far removed from slavery as to feel no personal or pecuniary interest in it, and who had known little save the darker side of the evil :

Up the hillside, down the glen,
Rouse the sleeping citizen;
Summon out the might of men!

Like a lion growling low,—
Like a night-storm rising slow,—
Like the tread of unseen foe,—

It is coming,—it is nigh!
Stand your homes and altars by;
On your own free thresholds die.

Clang the bells in all your spires;
On the gray hills of your sires
Fling to Heaven your signal-fires.

From Wachuset, lone and bleak,
Unto Berkshire's tallest peak,
Let the flame-tongued heralds speak.

O, for God and duty stand,
Heart to heart and hand to hand,
Round the old graves of the land.

Whoso shrinks or falters now,
Whoso to the yoke would bow,
Brand the craven on his brow !

*   *   *   *   *

"Make our Union-bond a chain,
  Weak as tow in Freedom's strain,
  Link by link shall snap in twain.

"Vainly shall your sand-wrought rope
  Bind the starry cluster up,
  Shattered over heaven's blue cope!

"Give us bright though broken rays,
  Rather than eternal haze,
  Clouding o'er the full-orbed blaze.

"Take your land of sun and bloom;
  Only leave to Freedom room
  For her plough, and forge, and loom;

     *   *   *   *   *

"Boldly, or with treacherous art,
  Strike the blood-wrought chain apart;
  Break the Union's mighty heart;

"Work the ruin, if ye will;
  Pluck upon your heads an ill
  Which shall grow and deepen still.

     *   *   *   *   *

"We but ask our rocky strand,
  Freedom's true and brother band,
  Freedom's strong and honest hand,-

"Valleys by the slave untrod,
  And the Pilgrim's mountain sod,
  Blesséd of our fathers' God!"

Whittier was unable to understand how men could yield to expediency when Justice and Right were at stake. To his soul at white heat and strained to its utmost tension, the spectacle of men arguing that this or that though just was not politic and therefore should not be entertained was so appalling, that he scarcely knew how to frame words to utter his horror and indignation. In these lines, published in 1846, entitled "The Pine-Tree," we hear a voice issuing from a soul burdened by shame for the country and weighed down with pity and grief:

Lift again the stately emblem on the Bay State's rusted shield,
Give to Northern winds the Pine-Tree on our banner's tattered field.
Sons of men who sat in council with their Bibles round the board,
Answering England's royal missive with a firm, "THUS SAITH THE LORD!"
Rise again for home and freedom!—set the battle in array!—
What the fathers did of old time we their sons must do to-day.

Tell us not of banks and tariffs,—cease your paltry pedler cries,—

Shall the good State sink her honor that your gambling stocks may rise?

Would ye barter man for cotton?—That your gains may sum up higher,

Must we kiss the feet of Moloch, pass our children through the fire?

Is the dollar only real?—God and truth and right a dream?

Weighed against your lying ledgers must our manhood kick the beam?

O my God!—for that free spirit, which of old in Boston town

Smote the Province House with terror, struck the crest of Andros down!—

For another strong-voiced Adams in the city's streets to cry,

"Up for God and Massachusetts!—Set your feet on Mammon's lie!

Perish banks and perish traffic,—spin your cotton's latest pound,

But in Heaven's name keep your honor,—keep the heart o' the Bay State sound!"

Where's the MAN for Massachusetts?—Where's the voice to speak her free?—

Where's the hand to light up bonfires from her mountains to the sea?

Beats her Pilgrim pulse no longer ?—Sits she dumb in her
    despair ?—
Has she none to break the silence ?—Has she none to do
    and dare ?
O my God ! for one right worthy to lift up her rusted
    shield,
And to plant again the Pine-Tree in her banner's tattered
    field !

In the following strong stanzas we again
hear the prophet speaking. He has ascended
the mountain far above the dull, plodding,
self-absorbed millions; he has communed with
the Divine, and the possibilities for progress,
happiness and advancement which lie along
the path of any people who are ever loyal to
the demands of justice and humanity to all
are no less vividly impressed on his mind,
than the awful disaster which confronts those
who refuse to leave the " mess of pottage "
found in self-gratification, and who yield
allegiance to shortsighted selfism to the de-
triment of others. There is something very
fine and inspiring in these lines and, what is
still more important, they are as appropriate

to-day as they were when the words flew
from the brain of the poet, as sparks from
the white-hot iron under the hammer of the
smith :

Forever ours! for good or ill, on us the burden lies;
God's balance, watched by angels, is hung across the skies.
Shall Justice, Truth and Freedom turn the poised and
    trembling scale ?
Or shall the Evil triumph, and robber Wrong prevail ?
Shall the broad land o'er which our flag in starry splendor
    waves
Forego through us its freedom, and bear the tread of slaves ?

The day is breaking in the East of which the prophets told,
And brightens up the sky of Time the Christian Age of
    Gold;
Old Might to Right is yielding, battle blade to clerkly pen,
Earth's monarchs are her peoples, and her serfs stand up
    as men;
The isles rejoice together, in a day are nations born,
And the slave walks free in Tunis, and by Stamboul's
    Golden Horn!

*   *   *   *   *

The Crisis presses on us; face to face with us it stands,
With solemn lips of question, like the Sphinx in Egypt's
    sands!

This day we fashion Destiny, our web of Fate we spin;
This day for all hereafter choose we holiness or sin;
Even now from starry Gerizim, or Ebal's cloudy crown,
We call the dews of blessing or the bolts of cursing down!

By all for which the martyrs bore their agony and shame;
By all the warning words of truth with which the prophets
    came;
By the Future which awaits us; by all the hopes which cast
Their faint and trembling beams across the blackness of the
    Past;
And by the blessed thought of Him who for Earth's freedom
    died,
O my people! O my brothers! let us choose the righteous
    side.

"Ichabod" is one of the most withering blasts that ever leaped from the indignant heart of an aroused prophet-poet. Its spirit is wholly unlike that which characterizes most of Whittier's lines; but it is a creation of great power—in its way, one of the most terrible utterances to be found in our literature. And curiously enough it was aimed at a kinsman of the poet—a New England statesman who had once stood very high in the regard of Mr. Whittier, and for whose intellectual powers he ever entertained the greatest admiration. The circumstances which gave rise to this poem are interesting and may be briefly stated as follows: On the seventh of March, 1850, Daniel Webster delivered a famous speech which struck dismay to the hearts of all friends of abolition in the North. In this oration he argued that no further restrictions on the extension of slavery in the territories of New Mexico and California were needed; that colonization by free negroes should be encouraged; and that the Fugitive Slave Law must be obeyed. He further averred that the labors of the Abolitionists had served merely to fasten the institution of slavery more firmly than ever on the South. This address, strange as it may appear to persons who do not understand that conservatism is always ready to bulwark an outgrown wrong if it be enthroned in high places, was applauded by leading educators of Harvard and Andover colleges. Indeed, an address of congratulation was presented to Webster, signed by eight hundred prominent citizens of the Old Bay State, including Rufus Choate, William H. Prescott, Jared Sparks, and Professor C. C. Felton, of Harvard College. It was this speech of Webster's, falling as it did with crushing force upon the Abolitionists, that called forth these terrible lines from Whittier:

> So fallen! so lost! the light withdrawn
>   Which once he wore!
> The glory from his gray hairs gone
>   Forevermore!
>
> Revile him not,—the Tempter hath
>   A snare for all;
> And pitying tears, not scorn and wrath,
>   Befit his fall!
>
> O, dumb be passion's stormy rage,
>   When he who might
> Have lighted up and led his age,
>   Falls back in night.

Scorn! would the angels laugh, to mark
    A bright soul driven,
Fiend-goaded, down the endless dark,
    From hope and heaven!

Let not the land once proud of him
    Insult him now,
Nor brand with deeper shame his dim,
    Dishonored brow.

But let its humbled sons, instead,
    From sea to lake,
A long lament, as for the dead,
    In sadness make.

Of all we loved and honored, naught
    Save power remains,—
A fallen angel's pride of thought,
    Still strong in chains.

All else is gone; from those great eyes
    The soul has fled:
When faith is lost, when honor dies,
    The man is dead!

Then, pay the reverence of old days
    To his dead fame;
Walk backward, with averted gaze,
    And hide the shame!

In speaking of the origin of this poem
Whittier wrote: "My admiration of the

splendid personality and intellectual power of the great Senator was never stronger than when I laid down his speech and, in one of the saddest moments of my life, penned my protest. I saw, as I wrote, with painful clearness, its sure results,—the slave-power arrogant and defiant, strengthened and encouraged to carry out its scheme for the extension of its baleful system, or the dissolution of the Union, the guaranties of personal liberty in the free States broken down, and the whole country made the hunting ground of slave-catchers. In the horror of such a vision, so soon fearfully fulfilled, if one spoke at all, he could only speak in tones of stern and sorrowful rebuke." "This poem," observes Mr. Kennedy, "has been compared to Browning's ' Lost Leader '—

" ' Just for a handful of silver he left us,
Just for a riband to stick in his coat—

*　　*　　*　　*　　*

" ' He alone breaks from the van and the freemen,
    He alone sinks to the rear and the slaves.

*   *   *   *   *

" ' Deeds will be done—while he boasts his quiescence,
    Still bidding crouch whom the rest bade aspire;
  Blot out his name, then, record one lost soul more.' "

Of the poems composed in war time none is more stirring than " Ein' Feste Burg," which opens with these memorable lines :

We wait beneath the furnace-blast
  The pangs of transformation;
Not painlessly doth God recast
  And mould anew the nation.
    Hot burns the fire
    Where wrongs expire;
    Nor spares the hand
    That from the land
  Uproots the ancient evil.

The hand-breadth cloud the sages feared
  Its bloody rain is dropping;
The poison plant the fathers spared
  All else is overtopping.
    East, West, South, North,
    It curses the earth;
    All justice dies,
    And fraud and lies
  Live only in its shadow.

This poem was set to music and sung with tremendous effect during the early days of the civil war. After the Battle of Bull Run, the famous Hutchinson family of singers entered the lines of the Army of the Potomac, hoping to reinvigorate the drooping spirits of the Union soldiers with their patriotic songs. On singing the "Ein' Feste Burg," however, General McClellan requested them to leave the lines. The singers appealed to President Lincoln, and this poem was read by Secretary Chase to the president and cabinet; after which the president said: "It is just the kind of a song I wish the soldiers to hear." The cabinet voted unanimously in favor of its being sung in the army, and the singers were readmitted to the national camps.

Just here it is interesting to note the martial spirit which pervades many of Whittier's lines, and his fondness for military imagery. It was Nathaniel Hawthorne who humorously alluded to him as " A fiery Quaker youth to whom the Muse had perversely assigned a battle trumpet." This fondness for the imagery of war perplexed Whittier not a little, and more than once when referring to it he expressed the conviction that there was " somewhere in his make-up quite a dash of the blood of the old sea king of the ninth century." Of course, anything military was as foreign to the Quaker theory of life and practice as was the shedding of blood abhorrent to Whittier, the poet. Nevertheless, during the early days of the war many young Quakers laid aside their drab for the soldier's uniform. In northern New Jersey, for example, a Quaker regiment was raised of one thousand members, much to the grief and dismay of many old and staid pillars in the society of Friends. At one of its quarterly meetings, the martial occupation of these stray sheep brought forth severe criticism from a number of members; whereupon one sympathizer with those who had donned the blue arose and told a little story: " He said that his grandfather once had dealings with an obstreperous 'man of the world,' who provoked him until his patience was worn out. All at once he threw off his coat and laid it on the ground, saying, ' Lie there, Quaker, till I give this rascal his dues ! ' and then proceeded to give him a good drubbing."

The poet has given us a graphic pen picture of himself during the anti-slavery conflict in the following lines from " The Tent on the Beach " :

> And one there was, a dreamer born,
>   Who, with a mission to fulfill,
> Had left the Muses' haunts to turn
>   The crank of an opinion-mill,
> Making his rustic reed of song
> A weapon in the war with wrong,
> Yoking his fancy to the breaking-plough
> That beam-deep turned the soil for truth to spring and
>   grow.

Too quiet seemed the man to ride
   The winged Hippogriff Reform;
Was his a voice from side to side
   To pierce the tumult of the storm ?
A silent, shy, peace-loving man,
He seemed no fiery partisan
To hold his way against the public frown,
The ban of Church and State, the fierce mob's
   hounding down.

For while he wrought with strenuous will
   The work his hands had found to do,
He heard the fitful music still
   Of winds that out of dream-land blew.
The din about him could not drown
What the strange voices whispered down;
Along his task-field weird processions swept,
The visionary pomp of stately phantoms stepped.

Great excitement prevailed throughout the North when President Lincoln countermanded as premature General Fremont's proclamation of freedom to the slaves in Missouri belonging to those who had taken up arms against the Federal government. Whittier at once penned his memorable ode to John C. Fremont, in which occur these lines :

Thy error, Fremont, simply was to act
A brave man's part, without the statesman's tact,
And, taking counsel but of common sense,
To strike at cause as well as consequence.

* * * * * *

Still take thou courage! God has spoken through thee,
Irrevocable, the mighty words, Be Free!

A most interesting anecdote relating to the above verses is related by Mrs. Jessie Fremont. In September, 1863, she visited Amesbury in order to see the poet, who, at the time, was absent from his home. He, however, soon returned and she met him in a frank, enthusiastic manner, but did not disclose her identity—— But here I must let her describe the incident, as furnished to Mr. Packard for his " Life and Letters of Whittier " :

" I began by telling him he had strongly influenced my young life ; that I was but twenty-two when I cut from a newspaper and pasted in my prayer-book his ' Angel of Patience ; ' that the lines

were the hardest to get *by heart* I had ever
tried, for patience and submission were not
natural growths in my part of the country.

" 'Thy speech is Southern ; what is thy
name?'

" 'Not yet,' I said. 'I am Southern; but
let me tell you more first. I want to tell you
of your last, your greatest help to us both—
to me and, greatest, to my husband.'

" And then I told him as briefly as I
could how over thirty thousand men were
next day to break camp for active pursuit of
the enemy,—' the enemies of the Union, Mr.
Whittier.' It was Sunday evening; the
setting sun lit up the October colors of the
trees, and picked out the white of tents cov-
ering the many hills ; the men were hushed
into reverent stillness, for the bands played
the air, and then voices, swelling to thousands
on thousands, took up the familiar words:

Before that awful throne who could know
how soon he must appear? And why?
What good attained for which a man should
lay down his life?

" The day's mail was brought into the
General's tent. He had no heart to open it,
for his highest, dearest, purest hopes had
been flung back on him, and himself dis-
approved. But I, who was always the secretary and other-self, went on with the things
of every day, 'taking the burden of life
again ; ' and think of my reward when in the
New York *Evening Post* there met my eye
your inspired, prophetic words!

" Uplifted beyond the time of trial, I went
out with the paper to where, standing over
the fire—as he so often stood in lonely times
of suffering and dejection—was the General,
alone. I read him the whole. He was
speechless with increasing, overwhelming,
glorified feeling—transfigured. Taking the

paper and bending to read it, for himself, by the blazing logs, at length he said :

"'He speaks for posterity. I knew I was right. I want these words on my tomb-stone :

"'God hath spoken through thee,
Irrevocable, the mighty words, Be Free!'

Now I can die for what I have done.'

"Whittier had grasped my arm, and his eyes blazed. 'What is thy name?'

"'Fremont.'

"Without a word he swung out of the room, to return, infolding in his helping embrace a frail little woman, tenderly saying to the invalid he was bringing from her seclusion :

"'Elizabeth, this is Jessie Fremont—under our roof! Our mother would have been glad to see this day.'"

At length the long agony of suspense drew to a close. The fierce battle waged by the little Spartan band had given place to one of those profound awakenings which suggest the on-sweeping of a prairie fire. The arrogance of the government and the courts, probably, did more than the agitation of the abolitionists to precipitate the war; but there can be no doubt but that the shafts of Garrison, the eloquence of Phillips, the clarion voice of brave Parker Pillsbury, the fiction of Mrs. Stowe, the stirring songs of the Hutchinson family, the writings of Horace Greeley and, last but not least, the poems of Whittier and Lowell were tremendous educational forces, while the tragic fate of John Brown gave great additional impetus to the cause of abolition. When Sumter was fired on the North was electrified, and war grim and terrible ensued, during which the evil of slavery went down; with peace came a wider freedom than we had before recognized. Then the bosom of our poet swelled with reverent thanksgiving, while his heart was melted with pity for the misery, the heartaches, and the lives lost in the awful strife.   One day the news came that the amendment had passed, abolishing slavery in the United States, and Whittier, seated in a meeting-house of the Friends, at Amesbury, heard the glad clanging of the bells in celebration of the event. The hour was one of the most impressive of his life. He was in the humble sanctuary of his people worshipping God; the merry pealing of the bells brought the message of a triumph of justice such as he had scarcely dared to pray for; and his breast became tremulous with emotion, his brain throbbed with exultant thoughts—a great song of triumph and thanksgiving rose in his soul, a song destined to live as long as our language endures.   And that is how the following magnificent poem, known as "Laus Deo!" came to be written:

It is done!
Clang of bell and roar of gun
Send the tidings up and down.

How the belfries rock and reel!
How the great guns, peal on peal,
Fling the joy from town to town!

Ring, O bells!
Every stroke exulting tells
Of the burial hour of crime.
Loud and long, that all may hear,
Ring for every listening ear
Of Eternity and Time!

Let us kneel:
God's own voice is in that peal,
And this spot is holy ground.
Lord, forgive us! What are we,
That our eyes this glory see,
That our ears have heard the sound!

For the Lord
On the whirlwind is abroad;
In the earthquake he has spoken;
He has smitten with his thunder
The iron walls asunder,
And the gates of brass are broken!

Loud and long
Lift the old exulting song;
Sing with Miriam by the sea,
He has cast the mighty down;
Horse and rider sink and drown;
" He hath triumphed gloriously ! "

Did we dare,
In our agony of prayer,
Ask for more than He has done?
When was ever His right hand
Over any time or land
Stretched as now beneath the sun?

How they pale,
Ancient myth and song and tale
In this wonder of our days,
When the cruel rod of war
Blossoms white with righteous law,
And the wrath of man is praise!

Blotted out!
All within and all about
Shall a fresher life begin;
Freer breathe the universe
As it rolls its heavy curse
On the dead and buried sin!

It is done!
In the circuit of the sun
Shall the sound thereof go forth.
It shall bid the sad rejoice,
It shall give the dumb a voice,
It shall belt with joy the earth!

Ring and swing,
Bells of joy!   On morning's wing
Send the song of praise abroad!
With a sound of broken chains
Tell the nations that He reigns,
Who alone is Lord and God!

A MODERN APOSTLE OF LOFTY SPIRITUALITY.

"In time to be
Shall holier altars rise to Thee,—
Thy Church our broad humanity !

*   *   *   *   *

"A sweeter song shall then be heard,—
The music of the world's accord
Confessing Christ, the Inward Word !

"That song shall swell from shore to shore,
One hope, one faith, one love restore
The seamless robe that Jesus wore."

—*Whittier.*

"The world is growing better ; the Lord reigns; our old planet is wheeling slowly into fuller light. I despair of nothing good. All will come in due time that is really needed. All we have to do is to work—and wait."
—*Whittier, in Pickard's " Life and Letters."*

III. A Modern Apostle of Lofty Spirituality.

NTERESTING as is the New England poet when considered as a barefoot boy, as the inspired prophet of freedom, as the charming lyric poet and graphic delineator of New England life, and dear as he is to us as the simple and sincere man, it is as the true mystic or inspired teacher of the higher life that he appeals especially to the large and rapidly increasing number of persons who, along various lines of thought and experience, are being brought to-day into what is essentially a deeply spiritual attitude, although they feel little or no attraction toward the empty forms, creeds or dogmas which have so long claimed to constitute religion. The " voice of God within," or "the Inner Light," of Whittier is becoming a far greater reality to the conscience of our civilization than Mammon-worshipping and easy-going conventionalists imagine. On this point the late Mrs. Claflin observed :

" Mr. Whittier believed in following the Inner Light, and when he thought he was directed by that Inner Light, no power on earth could influence him to turn aside. If he decided to move at a certain moment of time, nothing could induce him to change his mind; no storm was severe enough to deter him from going on the train he had set his heart on. He used to tell a story of one of his friends as an illustration of the wisdom of being guided by and yielding to the Inner Light :

" 'I have an old friend,' he said, 'who followed the leadings of the Spirit, and always made it a point to go to meeting on First-day. On one First-day morning, he made ready for meeting, and suddenly turning to his wife, said, 'I am not going to meeting this morning; I am going to take a walk.' His wife inquired where he was going, and he replied: 'I don't know; I am impelled to go, I know not where.' With his walking-stick he started, and went out of the city for a mile or two, and came to a country house that stood some distance from the road. The gate stood open, and a narrow lane, into which he turned, led up to the house, where something unusual seemed to be going on. There were several vehicles standing around the yard, and groups of people were gathered here and there. When he reached the house, he found there was a funeral, and he entered with the neighbors, who were there to attend the service. He listened to the funeral address and to the prayer. It was the body of a young woman lying in the casket before him, and he arose and said: 'I have been led by the Spirit to this house; I know nothing of the circumstances connected with the death of this person; but I am impelled by the Spirit to say that she has been accused of something of which she is not guilty, and the false accusation has hastened her death.'

"'The friend sat down, and a murmur of surprise went through the room. The minister arose and said, ' Are you a god or what *are* you?' The friend replied: 'I am only a poor, sinful man, but I was led by the Inner Light to come to this house and say what I have said, and I would ask the person in this room who knows that the young woman now beyond the power of speech was not guilty of what she was accused of, to vindicate her in this presence.' After a fearful pause, a woman stood up and said: 'I am the person,' and while weeping hysterically, she confessed that she had wilfully slandered the dead girl. The friend departed on his homeward way. Such,' said Mr. Whittier, 'was the leading of the Inner Light.'"

The same writer makes with regard to Whittier's religious convictions the following interesting observations, which accord with the spirit of his religious poems:

"Mr. Whittier was a many-sided man and could adapt himself to any condition of mind. He had great warmth of affection for his friends; tenderness to the erring, and capacity for suffering with others, were marked traits in his character,—but he had always faith in ultimate good for all. He said, 'Surely God would not permit His children to suffer if it were not to work out for them the highest good. For God never does, nor suffers to be done, but that which we would do if we could see the end of all events as well as He. The little circumstance of death will make no difference with me; I shall have the same friends in that other world that I have here; the same loves and aspirations and occupations. If it were not so, I should not be myself, and surely I shall not lose my identity. God's love is so infinitely greater than mine, that I cannot fear for His children, and when I long to help some poor, suffering, erring fellow-creature, I am consoled with the thought that His great heart of love is more moved than mine can be, and so I rest in peace.'"

How beautifully are these thoughts of the poet amplified in the following stanzas from "The Eternal Goodness":

> But still my human hands are weak
>   To hold your iron creeds:
> Against the words ye bid me speak
>   My heart within me pleads.

Who fathoms the Eternal Thought?
  Who talks of scheme and plan?
The Lord is God! He needeth not
  The poor device of man.

I walk with bare, hushed feet the ground
  Ye tread with boldness shod;
I dare not fix with mete and bound
  The love and power of God.

Ye praise His justice; even such
  His pitying love I deem:
Ye seek a king; I fain would touch
  The robe that hath no seam.

Ye see the curse which overbroods
  A world of pain and loss;
I hear our Lord's beatitudes
  And prayer upon the cross.

*   *   *   *

Yet, in the maddening maze of things,
  And tossed by storm and flood,
To one fixed trust my spirit clings;
  I know that God is good!

Not mine to look where cherubim
  And seraphs may not see,
But nothing can be good in Him
  Which evil is in me.

111

The wrong that pains my soul below
   I dare not throne above;
I know not of His hate,—I know
   His goodness and His love.

      *   *   *   *

And so beside the Silent Sea
   I wait the muffled oar;
No harm from Him can come to me
   On ocean or on shore.

I know not where His islands lift
   Their fronded palms in air;
I only know I cannot drift
   Beyond His love and care.

The true mystic is further revealed in the following verses from "In Quest":

" The riddle of the world is understood
   Only by him who feels that God is good,
   As only he can feel who makes his love
   The ladder of his faith, and climbs above
   On th' rounds of his best instincts; draws no line
   Between mere human goodness and divine,
   But, judging God by what in him is best,
   With a child's trust leans on a Father's breast,
   And hears unmoved the old creeds babble still
   Of kingly power and dread caprice of will,

Chary of blessing, prodigal of curse,
The pitiless doomsman of the universe.
Can Hatred ask for love?   Can Selfishness
Invite to self-denial?   *Is He less*
Than man in kindly dealing?   Can He break
His own great law of fatherhood, forsake
And curse His children?   Not for earth and heaven
Can separate tables of the law be given.
No rule can bind which He himself denies;
The truths of time are not eternal lies."

So heard I; and the chaos round me spread
To light and order grew; and, "Lord," I said,
"Our sins are our tormentors, worst of all
Felt in distrustful shame that dares not call
Upon Thee as our Father.   We have set
A strange god up, but Thou remainest yet.
All that I feel of pity, Thou hast known
Before I was; my best is all Thy own.
From Thy great heart of goodness mine but drew
Wishes and prayers; but Thou, O Lord, wilt do,
In Thy own time, by ways I cannot see,
All that I feel when I am nearest Thee!"

Whittier stood in the midway between the departing ideals of ancient orthodoxy and the religion of the future.   This is well illustrated in that exquisite poem, "The Brother of Mercy," which the reader will remember describes the death of one Piero Luca, an old, gray porter, who for forty years had wrought deeds of love and kindness. When the hour came and the lengthened shadows marked the close of life's day, a barefoot monk seeks thus to comfort the humble, Christ-lit soul of the dying man:

"My son,"
The monk said soothingly, "thy work is done;
And no more as a servant, but the guest
Of God thou enterest thy eternal rest.
No toil, no tears, no sorrow for the lost
Shall mar thy perfect bliss. Thou shalt sit down
Clad in white robes, and wear a golden crown
Forever and forever."

The following lines in a very real way reflect the poet's aversion to the ancient and materialistic conception of God and heaven, no less than his ideals of true religion, which the Apostle James cogently summarized as consisting in visiting the fatherless and widows in their affliction, and keeping one's self unspotted from the world:

Piero tossed

On his sick-pillow : " Miserable me !
I am too poor for such grand company ;
The crown would be too heavy for this gray
Old head ; and God forgive me if I say
It would be hard to sit there night and day,
Like an image in the Tribune, doing naught
With these hard hands, that all my life have wrought,
Not for bread only, but for pity's sake.
I'm dull at prayers : I could not keep awake,
Counting my beads.   Mine's but a crazy head,
Scarce worth the saving, if all else be dead.
And if one goes to heaven without a heart,
God knows he leaves behind his better part.
I love my fellow-men ; the worst I know
I would do good to.   Will death change me so
That I shall sit among the lazy saints,
Turning a deaf ear to the sore complaints
Of souls that suffer ?   Why, I never yet
Left a poor dog in the *strada* hard beset,
Or ass o'erladen !   Must I rate man less
Than dog or ass, in holy selfishness ?
Methinks (Lord, pardon, if the thought be sin !)
The world of pain were better, if therein
One's heart might still be human, and desires
Of natural pity drop upon its fires
Some cooling tears."

                Thereat the pale monk crossed
His   brow,   and,   muttering,   " Madman !   thou   art
  lost !"

Took up his pyx and fled ; and, left alone,
The sick man closed his eyes with a great groan
That sank into a prayer, " Thy will be done !"
    Then was he made aware, by soul or ear,
Of somewhat pure and holy bending o'er him,
And of a voice like that of her who bore him,
Tender and most compassionate: " Never fear !
For heaven is love, as God himself is love ;
Thy work below shall be thy work above."
And when he looked, lo ! in the stern monk's place
He saw the shining of an angel's face !

The poet's religious ideals are exquisitely
set forth in these stanzas :

O Love Divine !—whose constant beam
    Shines on the eyes that will not see,
And waits to bless us, while we dream
    Thou leavest us, because we turn from thee !

All souls that struggle and aspire,
    All hearts of prayer by thee are lit ;
And dim, or clear, thy tongues of fire
    On dusky tribes and twilight centuries sit.

*   *   *   *   *

Truth which the sage and prophet saw,
    Long sought without, but found within,
The law of Love beyond all law,
    The Life o'erflooding mortal death and sin !

116

The present broadening of man's ideas concerning God is seen on every side, both within and without the Church. The realization that empty dogma and soulless creed are no more religion than they were when Jesus condemned the scribes and Pharisees of old, is taking possession of the conscience of our civilization, at least of those who hunger and thirst after truth. Whittier thus anticipated the noble views which to-day are coming to be so generally accepted : *

> Above, below, in sky and sod,
>   In leaf and spar, in star and man,
>   Well might the wise Athenian scan
> The geometric signs of God,
>   The measured order of His plan.
>
> And India's mystics sang aright
>   Of the One Life pervading all,—
>   One Being's tidal rise and fall
> In soul and form, in sound and sight,—
>   Eternal outflow and recall.

*　　*　　*　　*　　*

* The Over-Heart.

Fade, pomp of dreadful imagery
  Wherewith mankind have deified
  Their hate, and selfishness, and pride !
Let the scared dreamer wake to see
  The Christ of Nazareth at his side !

What doth that holy Guide require ?—
  No rite of pain, nor gift of blood,
  But man a kindly brotherhood,
Looking, where duty is desire,
  To Him, the beautiful and good.

One would almost imagine the Quaker poet had been drinking from the fountain of Eastern mysticism, after reading these verses from " A Mystery " :

A presence, strange at once and known,
  Walked with me as my guide ;
The skirts of some forgotten life
  Trailed noiseless at my side.

Was it a dim-remembered dream ?
  Or glimpse through æons old ?
The secret which the mountains kept
  The river never told.

But from the vision ere it passed
  A tender hope I drew,
And, pleasant as a dawn of spring,
  The thought within me grew,

That love would temper every change,
    And soften all surprise,
And, misty with the dreams of earth,
    The hills of Heaven arise.

No poet of our time has been a firmer believer in the present, or in the splendid future to which mankind is slowly but laboriously tending, than was Whittier. The very keynote of his inspired conviction was sounded in the "Chapel of the Hermits" in the following utterances:

Yet, sometimes glimpses on my sight,
Through present wrong, the eternal right;
And step by step, since time began,
I see the steady gain of man;

That all of good the past hath had
Remains to make our own time glad,
Our common daily life divine,
And every land a Palestine.

*   *   *   *   *

O friend! we need nor rock nor sand,
Nor storied stream of Morning-Land;
The heavens are glassed in Merrimack,—
What more could Jordan render back?

We lack but open eye and ear
To find the Orient's marvels here;—
The still, small voice in autumn's hush,
Yon maple wood the burning bush.

For still the new transcends the old,
In signs and tokens manifold;—
Slaves rise up men; the olive waves,
With roots deep set in battle graves !

Through the harsh noises of our day
A low, sweet prelude finds its way;
Through clouds of doubt, and creeds of fear,
A light is breaking, calm and clear.

That song of Love, now low and far,
Erelong shall swell from star to star!
That light, the breaking day, which tips
The golden-spired Apocalypse !

With equal clearness were his beliefs as regards duty expressed in these lines from "Seed-Time and Harvest":

It may not be our lot to wield
The sickle in the ripened field;
Nor ours to hear, on summer eves,
The reaper's song among the sheaves.

Yet where our duty's task is wrought
In unison with God's great thought,

The near and future blend in one,
And whatsoe'er is willed, is done!

The poet's trust in the Over-Soul is frequently uttered, although at times there seems to be a wavering in the tones. When he is on the mountain top he is serene, and then we find him unmoved in his profound conviction. Thus, in the little poem entitled "Trust," he exclaims :

"All is of God that is, and is to be;
And God is good." Let this suffice us still,
Resting in childlike trust upon His will
Who moves to His great ends unthwarted by the ill.

To a correspondent in 1881 he wrote : "The world is growing better; the Lord reigns; our old planet is wheeling slowly into fuller light. I despair of nothing good. All will come in due time that is really needed. All that we have to do is to work—and wait." And again, in "The Grave by the Lake," after giving us an exquisite picture of lake and sky, mingled with philosophy and musings, he breaks forth much as did the elder prophets, speaking with the authority of one who is moved by a lofty inner voice:

Hear'st thou, O of little faith,
What to thee the mountain saith,
What is whispered by the trees ?—
" Cast on God thy care for these;
Trust Him, if thy sight be dim :
Doubt for them is doubt of Him.

*   *   *   *   *

" Not with hatred's undertow
Doth the Love Eternal flow;
Every chain that spirits wear
Crumbles in the breath of prayer;
And the penitent's desire
Opens every gate of fire.

" Still Thy love, O Christ arisen,
Yearns to reach these souls in prison!
Through all depths of sin and loss
Drops the plummet of thy cross!
Never yet abyss was found
Deeper than that cross could sound!"

Therefore well may Nature keep
Equal faith with all who sleep,

Set her watch of hills around
Christian grave and heathen mound,
And to cairn and kirkyard send
Summer's flowery dividend.

It was given to Whittier to see the unity of truth. He could never have been a Calvinist, and I say this without the least disrespect for the sincere leader of a great movement which aimed to purify the Church, although, from my point of view, in spite of the purity of his motive, Calvin dwelt in the shadow, while Whittier lived in the sunlight of spirituality. Calvin was naturally narrow in his views ; Whittier also had his limitations, but in the latter there are an inspiration and breadth which lead the soul upward, and radiate that largeness of spirit for the want of which any civilization or religion must wither. Thus, in the following lines,* the poet asserts a saving spaciousness of thought that, universally accepted and acted on,

* Miriam.

would do more than we can comprehend toward advancing brotherhood throughout the world:

> Truth is one;
> And, in all lands beneath the sun,
> Whoso hath eyes to see may see
> The tokens of its unity.
> No scroll of creed its fulness wraps,
> We trace it not by school-boy maps,
> Free as the sun and air it is
> Of latitudes and boundaries.
> In Vedic verse, in dull Korán,
> Are messages of good to man;
> The angels to our Aryan sires
> Talked by the earliest household fires;
> The prophets of the elder day,
> The slant-eyed sages of Cathay,
> Read not the riddle all amiss
> Of higher life evolved from this.

*　　*　　*　　*　　*

> Wherever through the ages rise
> The altars of self-sacrifice,
> Where love its arms has opened wide,
> Or man for man has calmly died,
> I see the same white wings outspread
> That hovered o'er the Master's head !

*　　*　　*　　*　　*

So welcome I from every source
The tokens of that primal Force,
Older than heaven itself, yet new
As the young heart it reaches to,
Beneath whose steady impulse rolls
The tidal wave of human souls;
Guide, comforter, and inward word,
The eternal spirit of the Lord!
Nor fear I aught that science brings
From searching through material things;
Content to let its glasses prove,
Not by the letter's oldness move,
The myriad worlds on worlds that course
The spaces of the universe;
Since everywhere the Spirit walks
The garden of the heart, and talks
With man, as under Eden's trees,
In all his varied languages.

As the shadows of eventide fell over his form the things of life dropped more and more away, and the profound trust that had been his stay through life filled his soul with a great calm. In a letter to Oliver Wendell Holmes, written in 1879, we find him thus reiterating his convictions: "I realize more and more that *fame and notoriety can avail little in our situation; that love is the one essential thing, always welcome, outliving time and change, and going with us into the unguessed possibilities of death.   There is nothing so sweet in the old Bible as the declaration that 'God is love.'"*

In closing this sketch of the life of a true mystic, I cannot do better than quote from Mrs. Claflin's "Recollections":

"If the worth of a life may be estimated by the number of hearts comforted, the number of lives uplifted and inspired, Mr. Whittier's measure will exceed that of most men of this or any other century.   'He has given us the poetry of human brotherhood and human purity.   He has given us a Christ-like example.   He has sung to us of faith in God and immortality.'

"The beautiful life finished its earthly course on a perfect summer's morning, and he entered the life for which he longed.

His last words were characteristic. He was breathing out his life ; his eyes were closed, and his friends stood around the bed about which had clustered so much loving interest, waiting and watching for the last look, or the last word, when he opened those eyes which had often seemed to look into the mysteries of eternity, and said with labored breath, ' My — love — to — the — world.' "

As we see with broader vision, we appreciate more and more the catholicity of Whittier, and that true spirituality which is expressed in deeds rather than in creeds—and which is yet to redeem the world.

THE MAN.

" In the habit as he lived."

—Shakespeare.

" Like warp and woof all destinies
    Are woven fast,
Linked in sympathy like the keys
    Of an organ vast.

" All which is real now remaineth,
    And fadeth never :
The hand which upholds it now sustaineth
    The soul forever."

—Whittier.

IV. The Man.

THE life of Whittier, like that of Emerson, was beautiful in its simplicity and naturalness. Aside from the conspicuous absence of the spectacular or dramatic element in his make-up, there was a marked freedom from that pernicious artificiality which permeates modern life and exalts the letter while it ignores the spirit. The sincerity and transparency of his life add greatly to the positive inspiration from which posterity for ages to come will imbibe high, fine truths, as from a mighty limpid reservoir,—truths which, like the teachings of the great Galilean, are so simply clad that they appeal to the unlettered, no less than to the spiritually minded among scholars.

It is good to draw very near to such a life, in the same way as it is helpful to journey forth into the country in springtime, when Nature is awaking, and on every hand one feels an indefinable uplift born of the glory of new life and its promised fruition.

Mrs. Mary B. Claflin, one of the poet's most intimate friends, in writing of Whittier says : *

"With him duty was commanding, and he always kept before him and acted upon the idea that ' beyond the poet's sweet dream lies the eternal epic of the man.'"

It is necessary to note here, however, that after the war of the Rebellion the poet ceased to be, in a marked degree, an aggressive reformer.   True, his instincts were ever on the side of justice, freedom, and progress ; but after the emancipation of the slaves he

* " Personal Recollections of Whittier."

laid aside the warrior's coat of mail for the quiet Quaker garb, if I may use these objective terms to illustrate mental conditions. This has been to me a source of deep regret; yet who shall judge, when the point at issue is merely a conviction of what is right? Moreover, I can well understand the poet's feelings, and it is but just that we examine him from his own point of view when discussing this change, which so boldly contrasted with the after life of so heroic a soul as Wendell Phillips.

Whittier had made a noble sacrifice when he cheerfully surrendered his cherished dream of political preferment and literary success, and cast in his lot with the little despised band of abolitionists, in conformity with what he conceived to be Duty's august demand. At the time of this great renunciation no epithets were too abusive, no ridicule was too cutting, no slander or calumny too gross to be meted out by easy-going conventionalists to the little band who seemed to be in a hopeless minority, but who bravely stood " on duty's vantage ground." After his decision had been deliberately made he fought valiantly nor faltered once, until the great cause to which he had consecrated his best energies was won, and the despised and persecuted minority became illustrious in the eyes of the majority.

Then, and not till then, the strong desire for peace and rest, and an intense longing to be able to ascend the mountain beyond the range of the fierce tumult below, over-mastered the aggressive spirit which was peculiarly prominent in the early years of Whittier's life. Moreover, it must not be forgotten that he was at once reformer and Quaker; the traditions of his people and a strong inward desire led him to seek that repose which aids in the development of spirituality. If Whittier had in him much of the crusader, he also possessed in a large way the soul which has ever dominated the oriental mystics and sages; indeed, the blending of these two elements in him was very marked. From his soul could flash that divine indignation which must have lit up Jesus' eyes when he overturned the tables of the money changers who had taken possession of his Father's temple; and yet few natures so yearned for peace and harmony, found only on the sunlit mountain peaks of love. From his luminous heart flowed the spirit of divine gentleness, compassion, and love of humanity, which was voiced in so characteristic an expression as his dying message, no less than in such typical lines as the following taken from his poem entitled " Worship ":

> O brother man ! fold to thy heart thy brother;
>   Where pity dwells, the peace of God is there;
> To worship rightly is to love each other,
>   Each smile a hymn, each kindly deed a prayer.

* * * * *

Love shall tread out the baleful fire of anger,
　　And in its ashes plant the tree of peace !

And in these typical stanzas from a poem written to be read at the levee given by the president of Brown University, June 29, 1870:

I touched the garment-hem of truth,
　　Yet saw not all its splendor.

＊　　＊　　＊　　＊　　＊

And slowly learns the world the truth
　　That makes us all thy debtor,
That holy life is more than writ,
　　And spirit more than letter.

＊　　＊　　＊　　＊　　＊

For truth's worst foe is he who claims
　　To act as God's avenger,
And deems, beyond his sentry beat,
　　The crystal walls in danger.

There is another fact which should be remembered when we are considering the change which marks Whittier as the prophet of freedom on the one hand and the poet of the *inner light* on the other, and that is

his almost incessant invalidism—insomnia
and neuralgia were the poet's familiar companions. After a sleepless night he was
often heard to say to his intimate friends in
his quaint and semi-humorous way, "It is of
no use; the sleep of the innocent is denied
me; perhaps I do not deserve it." *

But it is not my present purpose to notice
Whittier psychologically so much as to view
him "in the habit as he lived;" and, therefore, passing over this profoundly interesting
study, we come to view him in his home life.

Few men have ever so thoroughly enjoyed

---

* One who has suffered as did Whittier can readily see
how a soul constituted like his would yearn for peace and
rest.

This chronic invalidism, while it frequently rendered it
impossible for him to enjoy intercourse with kindred souls
and prevented him from attending public gatherings in
which he felt a deep interest, failed to mar his sweet dis-
position, or to ruffle the calm of a soul at once so profoundly
spiritual and yet so thoroughly human as was his. What
would have embittered most persons only seemed to add to
the serenity of his spirit.

the companionship of their friends as did our Quaker poet, and had his health permitted he doubtless would have found in social intercourse much pleasure which under existing circumstances was denied him.

Ralph Waldo Emerson was a great favorite of Whittier, although their visits to each other were necessarily infrequent. On one occasion, described by Mrs. Claflin, when the poet and philosopher were out driving, Emerson pointed out a small unpainted house by the roadside and said, "There lives an old Calvinist in that house, and she prays for me every day. I am glad she does. I pray for myself." "Does thee?" said Whittier. "What does thee pray for, friend Emerson?" "Well," replied Emerson, "when I first open my eyes upon the beautiful world, I thank God that I am alive and that I live so near Boston." On another occasion Whittier was telling Emerson of an original and somewhat remarkable farmer whom he knew. The great transcendentalist became much interested and remarked, " That man would enjoy Plato." At a later date Emerson sent the poet a copy of Plato to be loaned to his friend. On returning it the farmer expressed the satisfaction he had derived from the volume, adding that " that Mr. Plato has a good many of my idees."

Longfellow, Lowell, and Nathaniel Hawthorne were among other distinguished literary contemporaries whose friendship Mr. Whittier greatly prized. With the latter, who it will be remembered was a man of moods, Whittier related to Mrs. Claflin the following personal experience, which, though humorous to the reader, must have been exceedingly embarrassing to the poet at the time : " Thee knows," said Whittier, " I am not versed in small talk; but I wanted to make a friendly call on Hawthorne, and one morning (it chanced to be an ill-fated morning for this purpose) I sallied forth, and on reaching the house was ushered into a lugubrious-looking room, where Hawthorne met me, evidently in a lugubrious state of mind. In a rather sepulchral tone of voice he bade me good-morning, and asked me to be seated opposite him, and we looked at each other and remarked upon the weather. Then came an appalling silence, and the cold chills crept down my back. After a few moments I said, 'I think I will take a short walk.' I took my walk, and returned and bade him good-morning, much to my relief, and I have no doubt to his."

Whittier was a man of strong soul-friendships. Many of his dearest friends (such as John Bright, for example) he loved through spiritual kinship, although not enjoying personal acquaintance, and it is safe to say that all over the world the humble and unpretentious singer of New England was loved as a brother, counsellor, and friend. In this connection Mrs. Claflin has recorded a delightful episode relating to the meeting of Dom Pedro and Whittier in the following words :

"When Dom Pedro, the Emperor of Brazil, was visiting Boston, he was invited one morning to a private parlor to meet some of the men who have made this city famous in the world of letters. As one after another was presented to him, he received each one graciously, but without enthusiasm. But when Mr. Whittier's name was announced his face suddenly lighted up, and grasping the poet's hand, he made a gesture as though he would embrace him, but seeing that to be contrary to the custom of the Friends, he passed his arm through that of Mr. Whittier, and drew him gently to a corner, where he remained with him absorbed in conversation, until the time came to leave. The Emperor, taking the poet's hand in both his own again, bade him a reluctant farewell, and turned to leave the room, but, still unsatisfied, was heard to say, 'Come with me,' and they passed slowly down the staircase, his arm around Mr. Whittier."

It seems to have been one of the "ironies of fate" that Whittier, the home-lover and a man preëminently domestic in his tastes, should have been denied the companionship of a congenial wife. Many have been the romances hinted at and which have been alleged to have entered into his early life. Probably the one best authenticated appeared some time after the poet's death in that strictly edited daily, the *Republican*, of Springfield, Massachusetts; although I have found it impossible to absolutely verify the authenticity of the story, it is so probable as well as so interesting, that I give it below as it appeared under the title of "Whittier's Secret":

142

"The residence of eighteen months in Hartford introduced him to a vigorous anti-slavery circle of higher culture and a more delicate refinement than any he had known, and within that circle, incarnated in a most lovely woman, he was to find his fate.

"Among the friends the biographer has mentioned Judge Russ, a man well known in that day for brilliant parts and a handsome person. The family was distinguished for beauty and brightness. Of those members whom Whittier knew, Mary, the oldest, married Silas E. Burrowes. Mrs. Burrowes died of consumption in New York in 1841, at the age of thirty-four. There survived only an unmarried daughter, Cornelia, and one son, Charles James Russ, who twenty years later was a prominent lawyer in Hartford.

"Cornelia, the youngest child, born in 1814, was but seventeen years old when she parted from Whittier in 1831. He was twenty-four.   The strong anti-slavery zeal of the family threw the two young people much together, and the clear brain and tender heart of the poet yielded to very uncommon charms.   One who saw her during the last year of her life describes her in this way :

" ' At twenty-eight Cornelia was a most beautiful woman.   She had dark blue eyes, like pansies, with long, dark lashes, black hair, and the most exquisite color.   If she was like the rest of the family, she was a very brilliant woman.'

" Judge Russ, who was a member of Congress in 1820, had died in 1832.   Of this Whittier probably heard through his friend Law, but that he ever heard of the death of Mary Burrowes or Cornelia there is no evidence.   When he was writing his letter of sympathy to the friends of Lucy Hooper, Cornelia was lying on her deathbed.   She had nursed her sister through her fatal illness, had imbibed the poison, and followed her in the April of 1842.

" The poem called ' Memories,' to which Whittier attributed a special significance, was written during Cornelia's last illness. He thinks of her as still bright and living, and when in 1888 he desired the poem to be placed at the head of his subjective verse, his heart was still true to her, but gave no token that he knew hers had ceased to beat.

" After Cornelia's death her papers passed into the hands of the only surviving member of her family, Charles James Russ, who died in 1861. At that time her private letters came into the hands of his widow, who destroyed most of them, but kept, from pure love of the poet, the precious pages in which Whittier had offered himself to her kinswoman. I have not myself read the letter, which is still in existence, but one who has read it, the present possessor, writes me as follows : ' The letter was short, simple, and manly, as you would know. He evidently expected to call next day and learn his fate.' Another who has seen the letter writes: ' It was somewhat stiff—such a letter as a shy Quaker lad would be likely to write, for that he was in spite of his genius. He begged her, if she felt unable to return his affection, to keep his secret, for he said, ' My respect and affection for you are so great that I could not survive the mortification if your refusal were known.'

" Cornelia Russ was sought in marriage by several distinguished persons, but she died unmarried and she kept Whittier's secret. His poem suggests that the stern creed of Calvin held them apart—a thing very likely to happen in Connecticut half a century ago ; but if he had known that she had changed her early connections for the more liberal associations of the Church of England he would have seen more distinctly 'that shadow of himself in her ' of which the poem speaks.

" Those who are familiar with 'Memories' will recall the 'hazel eyes' and 'light brown hair' which it commemorates, and fancy perhaps that there is some mistake. It is not likely that Whittier forgot the color of Cornelia's eyes or hair. In some effusive moment he had shown the poem to James T. Fields and Edwin P. Whipple. In 1850, when Cornelia had been dead eight years, they wished to publish it, and he was very reluctant. He had not outgrown his early passion, and before it was printed he undoubtedly changed a few descriptive words to screen the truth, it may be from Cornelia herself. She never saw it, but I think he died believing that she had.

" Rumors of this story reached me long ago, but I would not print a mere surmise, and by long and devious ways leading through probate offices and town registers, through church records and private papers, in a varied correspondence that has occupied two months, have I followed the story as I tell it."

Although denied a wife, Whittier enjoyed for a long period the very intimate companionship of his best-beloved sister, as well as the association of some other members of the little group who composed the home circle when he was "a barefoot boy." For his sister Elizabeth, however, he ever cherished the deepest affection. She had poetic talent and was a keen as well as a sympathetic critic. Early in the autumn of 1864 this sister passed upward, and in a letter to Lucy Larcom dated Sept. 3, 1864, the poet wrote : *

" I feel it difficult even now to realize all I have lost. But I sorrow without repining, and with a feeling of calm submission to the will which I am sure is best. If I can help

* " John Greenleaf Whittier ; Life and Letters." By S. T. Pickard. Vol. ii., p. 480.

it, I do not intend the old homestead to be gloomy and forbidding through my selfish regrets. *She* would not have it so. She would wish it cheerful with the ' old familiar faces' of the friends whom she loved and still loves. I hope thee and other friends will feel the same freedom to visit me as heretofore."

In October of the same year, Whittier wrote Grace Greenwood the following letter which brings us very near to the heart of the poet : *

" My dear sister's illness was painful and most distressing, yet she was patient, loving, and cheerful even to the last. How much I miss her ! how much less I have now to live for ! But she is at rest. Surely, few needed it or deserved it more, if it were proper to speak of *deserve* in that connection. A

* *Ibid.* Vol. ii., pp. 481, 482.

pure, generous, loving spirit was hers. I shall love all her friends better for her sake. The autumn woods are exceedingly beautiful at this time. I miss dear Elizabeth to enjoy them with me. I wonder sometimes that I can be cheerful and attend to my daily duties, since life has lost so much of its object. But I have still many blessings— kind friends and books, and the faith that God is good, and good only."

Running through many of Whittier's letters is a strain of quiet humor, an example of which is given by Mr. Pickard in the following passage :

" There was a report abroad early in '67 that Whittier was about to marry. He refers to this in a letter to Lucy Larcom of March 16. 'Credulity! thy name is woman. So thee believed that report almost ? Well, it may be true, but the first intimation of it came to me through the newspapers. *They* ought to know. I can't imagine how the report was started. It vexed me, but of course there was no help for it. It is the cruelest irony to congratulate a hopeless old bachelor, within one year of sixty, on such prospects. I don't know about this ' freedom of the press.' "

To another correspondent who had written him in regard to the same matter, the poet replied :

" The idea of offering matrimonial congratulations to a hopeless old bachelor trying to thread a needle to sew on his buttons ! As well talk of agility to a cripple or a rise of government stocks to a town pauper. Of course thee did not believe this silly story. I don't care much about it, but I should be sorry to have to read congratulations upon it by every mail. I wish the newspaper scamp who started it nothing worse than to be an old bachelor like myself or to have a wife like Mrs. Caudle."

Few persons outside the poet's circle of friends knew that he was color-blind. His biographer thus refers to this defect :

" Mr. Whittier had the misfortune to be color-blind in respect to the shades of red and green. But he thought he had an unusual appreciation of the yellows which fully compensated him for this defect. He saw no difference in color between a red apple and the leaves of a tree upon which it was growing. It was only the white or yellow rose that had for him any beauty except of form. He thought he enjoyed the splendors of an autumn landscape in a wooded country as much as the ordinary observer, especially if there was a fair admixture of yellow foliage. When he brought home bouquets of leaves it was noticeable that yellow greatly predominated. Perhaps his preference for the golden-rod as the national flower was partly due to its color. His mother discovered this optical defect, when as a little boy he was picking wild strawberries. He could see no difference between the color of the berry and the leaf. 'I have always thought the rainbow *beautiful,*' he once said with an amused smile, 'but they tell me I have never seen it. Its only color to me is yellow.' A reddish brown book was handed him on the cover of which were lines of bright scarlet, and he was asked to tell the colors as he saw them. He thought the book was a dark yellow, and the scarlet lines stood out to him as bright yellow."

As with other lives, he who studies that of Whittier will constantly come across facts which are perplexing. In his opinions he was what his friends termed " firm," his critics " set," and his enemies (for in the aggressive period of his life he made foes) "stubborn." Then, again, there was present that strange inward struggle between the Puritan and Quaker, the "Peter and the John," the occidental and the oriental. He was by turns a shrewd and somewhat narrow New Englander, and at other times a broad idealist and mystic. Yet, with all this, his life was so pure, transparent, and noble in purpose, and permeated with so childlike a simplicity, that the outgush of his soul best mirrored the man. Thus in his letters and poems we gain a fine insight into the character of the poet. His remarkable self-control in later years was due to self-mastery. Mr. Pickard observes:

"It would be a mistake to suppose that gentleness was a necessity of his nature; it was in reality the result of resolute self-control and the *habitual government of a tempestuous spirit. He was quick and nervous in movement, but never otherwise than dig-*

nified and graceful. In conversation he spoke slowly and with precision, hesitating occasionally without the slightest nervousness for the word he wanted. This must have been the result of his habit of self-restraint, which became his second nature. He religiously curbed his tongue, and said of himself that he was born without an atom of patience in his composition, but that he had tried to manufacture it as needed."

Perhaps few men of so fine and lofty impulses have ever felt more keenly their shortcomings than did Whittier. In a letter to a friend written in 1879 he uses these touchingly frank expressions:

" I have been looking over my life, and the survey has not been encouraging. Alas! if I have been a servant at all I have been an unprofitable one, and yet I have loved goodness, and longed to bring my imaginative poetic temperament into true subjection. I stand ashamed and almost despairing before holy and pure ideals."

Other mental states are shadowed forth quite as forcibly in various stanzas of which the following is a fair example:

> Better to stem with heart and hand
>   The roaring tide of life, than lie,
> Unmindful, on its flowery strand,
>   Of God's occasions drifting by;
> Better with naked nerve to bear
> The needles of this goading air,
> Than in the lap of sensual ease forego
> The godlike power to do, the godlike aim to know.

And again the following paraphrase of a Sanscrit maxim, entitled "The Inward Judge," reveals the firm conviction of the poet:

> The soul itself its awful witness is.
> Say not in evil doing " No one sees,"
> And so offend the conscious One within,
> Whose ear can hear the silences of sin
> Ere they find voice, whose eyes unsleeping see
> The secret motions of iniquity.

156

Nor in thy folly say " I am alone."
For, seated in thy heart, as on a throne,
The ancient Judge and Witness liveth still,
To note thy act and thought : and as thy ill
Or good goes from thee, far beyond thy reach,
The solemn doomsman's seal is set on each.

Another glimpse of the true poet and man
is found in these lines from " At Last " :

When on my day of life the night is falling,
   And, in the winds from unsunned spaces blown,
I hear far voices out of darkness calling
   My feet to paths unknown,

Thou who hast made my home of life so pleasant,
   Leave not its tenant when its walls decay;
O Love Divine, O Helper ever present,
   Be Thou my strength and stay!

      *   *   *   *   *

Some humble door among Thy many mansions,
   Some sheltering shade where sin and striving cease,
And flows forever through heaven's green expansions
   The river of Thy peace.

There, from the music round about me stealing,
   I fain would learn the new and holy song,
And find at last, beneath Thy trees of healing,
   The life for which I long.

His strong faith in God, in man, and in

the future is a very striking characteristic of Whittier. It tinges his poems and lights up his personal letters as the sun lights the passing cloud with splendor. Thus, in a letter to Lucy Larcom we find this strong conviction :

"As we glide down the autumnal slopes of life how the shadows lengthen and deepen, but 'in the even-time there shall be light.' 'Death,' said the heathen stoic, 'is according to nature, and nothing is evil which is according to nature,' and there is deep wisdom and consolation in his saying. But as Christians our trust is not alone in the steady sequence of nature, but in the tender heart of our Father and the infinite love revealed in His human manifestation."

And again this same lofty faith is found in these exquisite stanzas among other pieces :

O golden age, whose light is of the dawn,
And not of sunset, forward, not behind,

Flood the new heavens and earth, and with thee bring
All the old virtues, whatsoever things
Are pure and honest and of good repute,
But add thereto whatever bard has sung
Or seer has told of, when in trance and dream
They saw the happy isles of prophecy!
Let justice hold her scale, and truth divide
Between the right and wrong; but give the heart
The freedom of its fair inheritance.
Let the poor prisoner, cramped and starved so long,
At nature's table feast his ear and eye
With joy and wonder; let all harmonies
Of sound, form, color, motion, wait upon
The princely guest, whether in soft attire
Of leisure clad, or the coarse frock of toil,
And, lending life to the dead form of faith,
Give human nature reverence for the sake
Of One who bore it, making it divine
With the ineffable tenderness of God.
Let common need, the brotherhood of prayer,
The heirship of an unknown destiny,
The unsolved mystery round about us, make
A man more precious than the gold of Ophir,
Sacred, inviolate, unto whom all things
Should minister, as outward types and signs
Of the eternal beauty which fulfils
The one great purpose of creation, love,
The sole necessity of earth and heaven.

It has been observed that every one puts

much of himself into his work, and this is peculiarly true of a life so transparent and simple as that of Whittier. Thus, I think that nowhere can we come into closer relationship to the real man than by a careful perusal of his works. His familiar form has left us. His benign smile is no more seen, even among the small circle of his loved friends and companions; but his fine thoughts, his inspiring words, which reveal his real worth as well as the divine mind, remain to inspire, strengthen, and ennoble the present generation and those that are to come, while the remembrance that his was a pure life, devoid of the feverish artificiality which so marks our occidental civilization, lends additional force to his lofty thoughts. The life and work of one like Whittier are an inestimable blessing to mankind, and his influence will continue for ages to come, for his thought was at once permeated with love and in alignment with freedom, justice, and progress.

Gerald Massey: Poet, Prophet, and Mystic.

A study of the life and thought of England's Poet of the People.

BY B. O. FLOWER.

ILLUSTRATED BY LAURA LEE.

CRITICAL PRESS OPINIONS.

Mr. B. O. Flower's latest work is a scholarly discussion of the life and work of Massey, poet, prophet, and mystic. One of the feature chapters is that in which the author traces the points of resemblance between Massey and Whittier. There are frequent quotations from the poet, but they are none too frequent, since they reveal to us the inner life of the man. — *Daily Advertiser, Boston, Mass.*

A most appreciative and tender tribute to one of England's lesser but noble song writers. No such presentation of the poet's character and work has yet been seen on this side the water. — *Daily Traveler, Boston, Mass.*

A handsome volume, both in print and illustrations, which presents briefly, but pointedly, the life and work of Gerald Massey. Our author finds a striking resemblance between Massey and our own loved Quaker poet, Whittier. Both were tireless reformers, "passionately in love with the beauty in common life." Both hated injustice with all their powers of mind, with prophetic and intuitive insight as to coming events. They both " revealed beauties within and without the homes of the humble," and were fearless in denunciation of wrong-doing. The work is handsomely illustrated, but the text alone makes it an interesting and even charming book. Mr. Flower makes free quotations from the gems of many of Massey's inspiring songs, and brings out admirably the leading traits of character that shaped his life and inspired his writing. — *Daily Inter-Ocean, Chicago, Ill.*

Price, extra cloth, gilt side and back dies, $1.00.

Arena Publishing Co., - Boston, Mass.

Civilization's Inferno

OR,

Studies in the Social Cellar.

By B. O. FLOWER.

This work contains vivid pen pictures of the social cellar as Mr. Flower found it, and is one of the most fearless and able presentations of the condition of society's exiles which has ever been made.

It carries the reader into the social cellar where uninvited poverty abounds, and from there into the sub-cellar, or the world of the criminal poor.

It is rich in suggestive hints, and should be in the hands of every thoughtful man and woman in America.

Absorbingly interesting and at times thrilling, no one can read its pages without being made better for the perusal.

CRITICAL OPINION FROM REPRESENTATIVE AMERICAN JOURNALS.

It is a truthful and graphic delineation of the condition of the people in the social undertow. Mr. Flower has a keen and profound sympathy with the difficulties that the poor are laboring under, and he describes what he has seen with his own eyes in terms that chill one's blood. He does not hesitate to call things by their right names, and points out the magnitude of the peril, showing that no palliative measures will satisfy the people. — *Daily Herald, Boston, Mass.*

Society, as it is now constituted, is nothing less than a sleeping volcano. Who dares to say how soon the upheaval will come, or whether it can be evaded by the adoption of prompt measures of relief? Certainly the condition of the lower social strata calls for immediate action on the part of those whose safety is at stake. Mr. Flower has accomplished a great work in setting forth the exact truth of the matter, without any effort at palliation. It will be well, indeed, for the prosperous classes of the community if they are warned in time. — *Boston Beacon, Boston, Mass.*

A thoughtful work by a thoughtful man, and should turn the minds of many who are now ignorant or careless to the condition of the countless thousands who live in the "social cellar." No one can read the book without feeling that the author's diagnosis of the case is true and gives each one his own personal responsibility. — *Courier-Journal, Louisville, Ky.*

What General Booth has done for London, and Mr. Jacob Riis for New York, Mr. Flower has done for cultured Boston. He is a professional man of letters, and tells his story with the skill and knack of his craft. — *Daily Constitution, Atlanta, Ga.*

Cloth, $1.00.   Paper, 50 cents.

Arena Publishing Co.,   -   Boston, Mass.